R OF WANDS

A NOVEL

MACKENZIE FLOHR

INDIGO

Livonia, Michigan

Edited by Lisa McNeilley and Morgan Smith
Proofreading by Jacquie New and Amanda Lewis

THE RITE OF WANDS

Published by Indigo
an imprint of BHC Press

Library of Congress Control Number:
2016962818

ISBN Numbers:
Softcover: 978-1-946006-43-1
Hardcover: 978-1-946848-86-4
Ebook: 978-1-948540-13-1

Visit the publisher at:
www.bhcpress.com

To those whom have been present
during my writing journey, thank you
for supporting and believing in me.

Without all of you,
none of this would have been possible.

Pronunciations of the Warlock Language

follows the Spanish alphabet

Aboterrar - (Ah bote rah)
Arduescha ridícula - (Are do eshca ree dee coo la)
Brujahvin - (Bru ha veen)
Convosurí - (Con vo sue ree)
Curtreforéa draco machado -
(Cur tre for e ah draco ma cha do)
Doltedormira - (Dol te door mee rah)
Draciolamus - (Drac see o la moose)
Emaculavi el curpas y mehartis -
(Eh ma coo la vee L coor pas ee meh har tees)
Esallertis - (Eh sa jer tees)
Fedish ramtatí - (Fedish ra ma ta tee)
Forina olivet - (Foreena olviet)
Gañoth - (Ga yeoth)
Gulpe ursígo - (Ghoul peh oor see go)
Kibunika lac due flambé -
(Ki boo nika lock due flam bay)
Klaocala - (Claou ca la)
Mostravit - (Mostra veet)
Nexeus - (Nex e us)

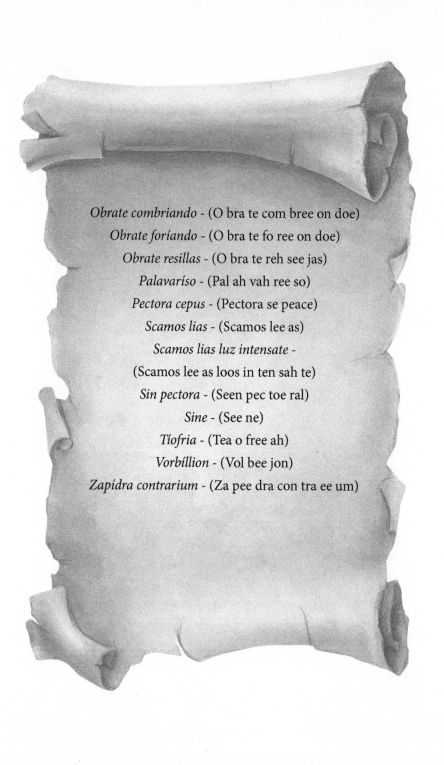

Obrate combriando - (O bra te com bree on doe)

Obrate foríando - (O bra te fo ree on doe)

Obrate resillas - (O bra te reh see jas)

Palavaríso - (Pal ah vah ree so)

Pectora cepus - (Pectora se peace)

Scamos lias - (Scamos lee as)

Scamos lias luz intensate -

(Scamos lee as loos in ten sah te)

Sin pectora - (Seen pec toe ral)

Sine - (See ne)

Tíofria - (Tea o free ah)

Vorbíllion - (Vol bee jon)

Zapídra contrarium - (Za pee dra con tra ee um)

HOW TO READ
ORLYND'S DIALECT

Ah = I	git = get
Ah hudnae even goat a deck at = to get a look at	goat = got
	hame = home
Ah'd = I'd	hudnae = had not
Ah'm = I am	huv = have
Ah says nae mair = I say no more	intae = into
	jist = just
Ah've = I have	ma = my
ain = way	mair = more
ay = of	n = and
deck = look at	nae = not
dinnae = don't	oan = on
eywis = these	oor = our
fi = from	tae = to
fir = for	thair = their
gen up = really?	they = those

thir = there

thit = that

whit = what

wi = with

wid = would

wis = was

yir = you're

yis = you

When dual warlocks of royal blood
reflect their image,
A time of great peril will commence;
One who is coerced will seek
the betrayal of power;
The energy of magic will serve
the bearer who brings peace

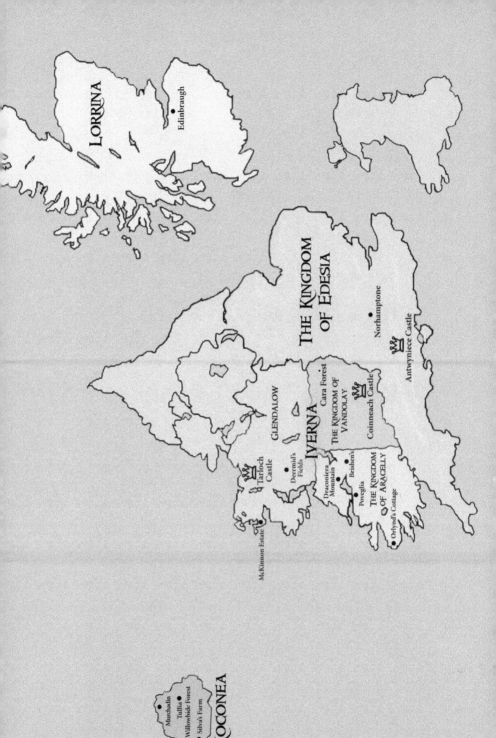

PART ONE

PART ONE

CHAPTER ONE

DRACONIERA MOUNTAIN
THE KINGDOM OF ARACELLY
1238 CE

Mierta McKinnon."

The twelve-year-old warlock gave a start, hearing his name announced telepathically. Mierta stood up on shaky legs and brushed his brown bangs out of his green eyes. The room inside Draconiera Mountain was suffocating. Hot springs bubbling up from deep beneath the ground created a dense fog, which pushed down on Mierta's shoulders. Sweat was already dripping from his brow onto his long, dark royal blue robe. His heart raced as he approached a large wooden door. He occasionally glanced over at others who were anxiously awaiting their turn, wondering which of those he made eye contact with would succeed.

No matter what happens. No matter what I see. I cannot allow my fears to overcome me, Mierta told himself. *I will achieve what I have come to do. I cannot fail. I won't. I will make Mother and Father proud.*

A loud creaking echoed across the room, and the ground shook underneath his feet. Two tall wooden doors opened up to a pathway of complete darkness.

"Step inside," he heard the dragon say. Mierta swallowed hard and expelled air through his mouth.

Upon entering the pathway, a warm mist rose from below. Water splashed against rocks, and occasional water droplets hit his skin. A faint glow shone in the near distance. He walked towards the glow until he found himself in a large, circular cavern. In the centre of this cavern was a short, round pedestal. An opening off towards the right looked like it was open-aired, and off to the left side was another doorway, which was currently closed.

Mierta gazed up at the source of the glow and caught a glimpse of the magnificent creature standing on a rocky ledge. He could hear his pulse beating in his ears. He felt as if his body was paralysed, yet he felt unsteady. His own rapid breathing masked the sound of Lord Kaeto stepping into the light.

Mierta gasped, shielding his eyes against the bright yellow light from Lord Kaeto's wings, trying to conquer his fear. When his eyes adjusted, he noted the ebony veins that traced a pattern, like the rivers in the valley. The veins seemed to pulse with power.

"Lord Kaeto," Mierta uttered, bowing, keeping his eyes averted to the ground.

Lord Kaeto was the last of his kind—an omniscient ancient breed of telepathic dragons that had been around for longer than any could remember. The residents of the kingdom looked at him as if he were a God, straight from the stories of old.

"Mierta McKinnon. Rise," he spoke. "It is your time to participate in the Rite of Wands in which your soul shall face the ultimate analysis. You will be taken on a journey of your lifetime, viewing portions of your past, present, and future. Do you accede?"

"Yes," Mierta answered, his voice breaking.

The Rite of Wands was a tradition among witches and warlocks when they reached their twelfth birthday. It was a ceremony which, once completed, would signify their initiation into the magical community, thereby allowing them to start practicing making potions and casting spells.

I will not fail. I cannot fail, Mierta recited to himself.

"Very well." Lord Kaeto nodded, pleased. "The Rite of Wands shall commence!"

Lord Kaeto tilted his head upwards and blew fire from his mouth.

Mierta lifted his hands to cover his face. When he heard the sound of the bolt slide open from the other side of the room, Mierta lowered his hands to watch as the door opened with a loud creak.

"Dragomir will be assisting me with the ritual," Lord Kaeto said as he looked toward the warlock who was entering the room.

Out stepped a warlock wearing tall black boots, a black tunic with a golden lacing, royal blue breeches and a long-sleeved white linen shirt. His face was hidden behind an orange and golden mask shaped like a dragon's head. The warlock raised his right hand into the air and shouted, *"Forina olivet!"*

A lightning bolt crashed down beside him, followed by the sound of drums beating, which gradually became louder until it matched every thump of Mierta's frantic heart.

While the door closed behind him, Dragomir walked to the edge of the room and bowed to the dragon. The drums stopped abruptly.

The warlock bowed his head toward Mierta.

Mierta glanced back, not reassured.

"His appearance may look frightening, but do not fear," Lord Kaeto continued. "I assure you he is only here to help me perform the magic, which is tiring for me. Now, Mierta, keep your eyes upon mine at all times. You may feel a tingling sensation as I investigate your essence." He turned toward the warlock. "Dragomir, you may begin. Wand at the ready."

Mierta watched Dragomir raise his wand and hold it out towards him. He took in a deep breath. He had heard stories about the Rite of Wands, but it was forbidden for anyone to discuss specifics of their individual ritual. The little knowledge he had told him the ceremony represented a kind of test before he would either be accepted as a full member of the magical community or not. If he failed, there would not be another chance; he would become a Magulia—a magical person without his or her powers. Magulians were looked down on and lived the remainder of their lives as outcasts.

The Rite of Wands began when Lord Kaeto entered his soul, though he did not know exactly what would happen. What he was about to see was a mystery, but how he endured would determine his fate.

When Mierta stared into Lord Kaeto's golden amphibian eyes, they were not frightful as he had expected. Instead, they appeared old and sad, as though he already knew what he was about to see. This sent a chill down Mierta's body.

Lord Kaeto could see what Mierta's heart desired. There was both good and evil inside him, caused by a deep hurt that had yet to be mended.

Please, do not curse me to a life without magic, Mierta begged.

At the same time Dragomir shouted, *"Fedish ramtatí!"*

It did not take long before Mierta started to feel the effects of the spell. First, he experienced what felt like a dozen small black bugs crawling up his skin. His mind urged him to scratch to rid his body of them. He reached out a hand to scratch his left arm, when suddenly Dragomir cast another spell. *"Gañoth!"*

Mierta abruptly stopped. A small *oooof* escaped his lips as he was promptly thrown backwards against the pedestal located directly behind him. He felt as if all the air was being released from his lungs, followed by intense pain, as though he had been punched in the stomach. Stars filled his vision.

Dragomir watched the young warlock's eyes start to roll. He pointed his wand straight at Mierta's heart and stepped in closely to deliver the final blow. There was no hesitation in Dragomir's movements or guilt in his eyes. He swung his hand around in a large circle and shouted, *"Draciolamus!"*

Mierta gasped and his eyes refocused. He was rewarded with air returning to his lungs. He took in several deep breaths, treasuring them as if they were to be his last. He closed his eyes and reopened them just in time to see a set of arms and hands appear, detached and demon-like. They were the colour of misty grey mixed with black. As the disembodied parts slithered toward him like a snake, a moaning sound emanated from them.

He must have cast a spell that causes hallucinations. Oh, how brilliant! I reckon as long as I don't give in to the fear, I will get through this, Mierta thought.

Mierta wanted to break the trance; however, he was determined not to show the dragon any weakness. One day, he was certain, he would become the most powerful warlock in Iverna. He would do wonders for the magical community while he sought vengeance for the crime committed against his mother.

His body trembled while the hands crawled up his legs. His pulse increased again, and his breathing became uneven once he felt them slip underneath his breeches. They climbed up his legs and made their way under his wool shirt until they reached his chest. Then they stopped.

"Lord Kaeto?" Mierta questioned, perplexed.

He let out a cry when he felt a sharp, stabbing pain. One of the hands had entered his body through the right side of his chest. Crying out again when the other hand followed through his left side, Mierta looked down to see a gruesome sight of blood saturating through his royal blue robe where the hands had entered him. He felt overly hot as blood rushed to his face and nausea built in his throat. Taking a step forward, he heard a squishing sound. He looked down to see blood had pooled at his feet.

"Lord Kaeto," Mierta uttered between breaths. "What?"

A high-pitched ringing filled his ears. The world before him rapidly spun and transformed into white puffy clouds. His eyes rolled into the back of his head and his knees buckled as the darkness engulfed him.

CHAPTER TWO

COINNEACH CASTLE
THE KINGDOM OF VANDOLAY
1238 CE

In the land of Iverna among vast farmland, deciduous woodland covered in wild garlic, and rocky meadows, resided a kingdom of men called Vandolay. Over time, the kingdom had become recognised for its obsequious and short-tempered king and its arrogant and no-nonsense prince, rather than its abundant wildlife, varied crops, and flourishing economy.

Tiberius paced in front of King Francis's private apartment where the King of Vandolay was enjoying some quiet time alone in the dining area.

"Your Grace, I've come to ask for...no, still not right. How did it go again?" Tiberius questioned with laboured breath, stopping abruptly to wipe his hands. He could hear his pulse pounding in his ears. He glanced down the hallway, taking note of the paintings by various artists, trying to calm himself. Sweat ran down his back underneath his deep red robe. He straightened the vestments of his religious attire and tried to stop his knees from knocking together. His footsteps echoed as he, again, nervously paced the stone floors. Sunlight shone through a narrow window highlighting his anguished face.

"How did whit go, Father?" Orlynd asked, filled with bewilderment. "Yis said His Grace wished tae see me."

"His Grace did not exactly say it, but do not fear, his mind will change. You brought your wand with you, did you not?" Tiberius questioned.

"Aye, but Ah dinnae understand?"

"Never mind," Tiberius interrupted. "It may be necessary to have." Tiberius returned to his rehearsed speech. "Your Grace, I've been blessed by God. Yes, that will be sufficient." He breathed deeply and placed his hand over the door lever. Certainly, if he could return to God's good graces after committing an unforgivable sin, so then, couldn't he once again find the king's forgiveness? He turned the lever and pushed, only to find it locked.

"Halt, right there!" yelled Thomas, one of the king's guards on duty, spotting Tiberius and Orlynd. "You cannot enter."

Tiberius and Orlynd stopped. Tiberius leaned in and whispered, "Orlynd, when you see me gesture to you with my hand, I need you to cast a charm on the lock to unlock His Majesty's private apartment. I will distract the guard."

"But, Father! Ah dinnae think…" Orlynd began.

Tiberius turned to see a young man dressed in a gold tunic with dark blue leggings underneath approaching them. The crest of the kingdom was on his breast.

"I beg your pardon?" Tiberius smiled with only the corners of his lips turned upward. He cleared his throat. The sound echoed down the hall.

A rush of heat travelled to Orlynd's face.

The guard narrowed his eyes. "The king is not to be disturbed."

Tiberius, smiling with a closed mouth, turned to the guard. He said politely, "Forgive me. I did not catch your name."

"Thomas," the guard answered matter-of-factly.

Tiberius concluded the best way to distract the guard was by means of reasoning. "Thomas, my good fellow, I believe there has been a misunderstanding. I seek an audience with His Grace. My son, Orlynd, has something of great value."

"Nae, Ah dinnae," Orlynd protested.

Tiberius raised his hand to silence his son.

Thomas briefly eyed the boy suspiciously, then glanced back at Tiberius. He continued, "There is no mistake, Your Eminence. His Majesty has stated you are not welcome in his court. You both must follow me now quietly or you'll be arrested for treason."

Orlynd felt his heart start to race at the announcement. "Father," he begged, fearing his father would cause further disgrace. "Please!"

Tiberius glared at his son. "Very well, then. Lead the way." Tiberius smiled in an annoying, self-satisfied manner. He took a few steps forward then stopped. He waited until the guard had turned his back towards them before gesturing to his son.

Orlynd's eyes grew wide as he watched his father make a fist with his right hand and rotate it around three times counterclockwise before bending his fist downward and stopping.

Orlynd shook his head.

Again, he was met with a scowl.

Orlynd felt sweat now dripping down the back of his robe. He did not have the courage to stand up to his father. He sighed deeply and nodded in defeat and removed from the inside of his robe a lignum vitae wooden wand with a Satya Mani Quartz crystal fused at the shaft. Turning to face the door, he pointed his wand towards the door lever. With a frown, he whispered, *"Obrate foriando."*

The sound of a lock unbolting met his ears. Shortly followed by the sound of obnoxious creaking as the door opened on its own.

Tiberius turned around, smiling approvingly. "Quickly, son!"

"Halt!" Thomas yelled, pursuing them.

They swiftly moved inside the king's private apartment.

The trio found themselves in a large room. The thick, richly decorated rug stretching from wall-to-wall muffled their footsteps as they entered. Heavy, royal red drapes hung from the top of the two floor-to-ceiling windows. These had been pulled back, and the windows hung open to allow a slight breeze to cool the room. The sparse furnishings included two writing desks and chairs made of a dark walnut wood.

Orlynd was most impressed with the quartet of floor-to-ceiling shelves, filled with books on either side of a doorway at the far end of the room. He could only imagine the stories and information contained within them.

The king, hearing the distraction, approached from another room, pulling on a long grey silk dressing gown with gold accents on the sleeves, and tying a belt around his waist. "What is the meaning of this?" He glared at his guard and sneered. His shoulder-length curly brown hair looked voluminous and slightly dishevelled. "Thomas, unless my memory has failed me, which it has not, I commanded you to keep the door locked."

The guard abruptly bowed to the king. "I am so sorry, Your Grace," Thomas said, stammering, trying to regather his composure. "I told them you were not to be disturbed. I made no mistake in locking the door. It was the boy, sir. He is a warlock."

The king raised a hand and silenced Thomas. He quickly glanced over at the boy and dismissed Thomas's accusation. Turning his attention to Tiberius, he spoke with an assertive, no-nonsense tone. "Tiberius O'Brien. I thought I had made myself clear. You and your family were to return to Edesia immediately."

"Yes," Tiberius said with an apologetic tone. "A thousand pardons, Your Grace. I wanted…"

"I should have you locked up in the dungeons of Tarloch Castle for your insubordination. How dare you disturb me while I am in my private chambers!"

Tiberius dropped to his knees and lowered himself to the ground, his oily black hair brushing the king's shoes. "Forgive me, Your Majesty! I beg of you. Please allow me to explain. I have found you a new advisor!"

Francis eyed the sixteen-year-old boy standing behind Tiberius. "What is this mockery? Do you take me for a fool, Chancellor?"

"No, Your Grace," Tiberius answered nervously as he raised himself from the ground and kissed the king's hand. "I assure you this is no jest."

Francis took in a deep breath, took another glance at the boy and studied his appearance. He looked nothing like the man standing beside him. He was thin, had ginger-brown hair and deep, piercing brown eyes. In fact, he reminded him more of himself when he was a young prince, minus the eyes and the hair.

Could he be? Nay, it is impossible.

The king's heart took a sudden thump as he was instantly reminded of one of his beloved advisors, Celeste, who had been considered a confidant and a close friend before she had passed unexpectedly.

This cannot be, yet the resemblance is uncanny. The boy's parentage is unquestionable.

Francis shot Orlynd a look. He had to scrutinise him to discover the truth. "What is your name, boy?" the king inquired.

"O…Orlynd, Yir Grace," Orlynd replied, between swallows. His throat closed up, preventing him from speaking. His breathing increased and sweat began to drip down the side of his face.

The king's eyes grew wide and his heart softened. He recognised the Lorritish burr of his former advisor, who was also from the nation of Lorrina. There could be no mistaking it now.

"You are Celeste's boy, are you not, Orlynd?" Francis asked.

"Aye," Orlynd confirmed, nodding his head. Orlynd didn't see why the king asked him the question; all he knew was that his mother had once served as advisor to the king.

The king turned in disbelief. He glanced upward, tears filling his eyes, recalling the smile on her face when she had informed him she was with child.

You were so happy, and I was delighted for you. I will never understand why you chose to hide the real truth from me!

Orlynd's heart began to race. Had he offended the king?

"Should I be rid of them, Your Grace?" Thomas questioned.

"Leave us!" the king abruptly shouted, startling Orlynd.

"Yes, Your Grace." Thomas bowed, speaking no further, and took his leave, shutting the door behind him.

The king composed himself and turned to Tiberius. "You are certain the boy has the gift?"

Tiberius smiled at Orlynd. "Yes, Your Grace."

Sudden warmth filled the king's heart. "Speak quickly and tell me everything you know," the king commanded.

Tiberius adjusted his collar. "Yes, well, I returned home after our last audience. I went into my study and found my son standing frozen, facing the wall, his eyes trancelike and fearful. A remnant of flames glowed in his pupils."

Francis folded his hands and let out a deep breath. "I want to believe you, but Celeste never had episodes such as this. If Orlynd is truly a soothsayer like you say, then he will have to prove it. The boy shall step forward."

Orlynd's jaw dropped.

How was he supposed to prove to the king he was a soothsayer? He couldn't control it by sheer will. Being a soothsayer wasn't a gift. It was a curse! He would fail. There was no way he could possibly prove it to either of them.

He looked back at his father with desperation.

Tiberius whispered in his ear. "Tell His Grace what you stated in the study, yeah?"

Orlynd nodded, noticing the king was quickly growing impatient.

"All right." Tiberius smiled. "Go on then."

Orlynd hesitated to move.

Tiberius responded by clearing his throat and nudging him forward.

Orlynd's heart raced. What if he couldn't remember what he said? What if the king didn't believe him? He so badly wanted to please his father. What if he let him down? He looked up into the face of the king.

"Well? Do you have something to say to me or not, boy?"

"A...aye, Yir Majesty," Orlynd stammered. "S...sorry, Yir Grace."

"For God's sake, spit it out, boy!"

The king watched him intently.

Orlynd closed his eyes and positioned his hands inside his brown robe. He blinked, lowering his head, then he opened his eyes, raised his head, and spoke confidently.

"When dual warlocks ay royal blood reflect thair image, a time ay great peril will commence. Oan who is coerced will seek the betrayal ay power; the energy ay magic will serve the bearer who brings peace."

Francis paused, deep in thought.

"Your Grace?" Tiberius said, questioning the king's hesitation.

"Never in the history of this kingdom has any member of the crown contained the blood of a warlock," he said, dismissing the prediction. "I fail to see the relevance of this."

"With all due respect, sire," Tiberius said. "I believe my son is delivering a message of warning. You know as well as I, it would not be difficult for a witch from the Kingdom of Aracelly to conjure up an enchantment to use on you and your son without your consents!"

"Silence!" the king snapped, his eyes blazing. "I do not seek your advice. I have already made a grave error allowing you to convince me to agree to the Vatican's plan of purging Iverna of Magulians. The crown is in danger and my people believe I have gone mad! I will hear no more."

"I urge Your Majesty to reevaluate!" Tiberius persuaded. "My son's gift is real. Orlynd can help restore Your Grace's honour."

"Tell me," Francis hissed. "Are Orlynd and the Vatican going to pay for the ships and supplies I lost in order to eradicate the Magulians? I think not." He had enough of Tiberius's nonsense. "Chancellor, I will personally arrange for the next carriage to take you back to Edesia immediately. You can pass your wisdom on to the Edesian church. You will never step foot in my castle again or heed my warning: I will not show you mercy. As for your son, Orlynd, I have decided…"

Orlynd lowered himself to the ground as the king turned his back. "Ah beg ay yir forgiveness, Yir Grace!"

The king stopped, shocked by Orlynd's reaction. "Orlynd. Rise," Francis commanded, waiting till the warlock stood back up. "Never throw yourself at my feet again. You need only bow."

Orlynd nodded, tearfully.

Perhaps he has the gift or perhaps not. Time will unravel the truth, but keep him near in honour of Celeste, I shall, Francis thought to himself.

"Orlynd O'Brien," the king continued, "I appoint you as my new advisor. You shall serve my family just as your mother did."

Orlynd stared at the king with disbelief. "Thank yis, Yir Grace."

The king continued. "I will arrange new quarters for you here at court. You shall have everything you will ever need as long as you stay in my good graces. I will look to you as my conscience and as my friend. This is your home now."

Orlynd carefully listened to the king's instructions.

"As for your father, he must pay for his sins." Francis looked at Tiberius. "He has shamed his family name. This is a burden you must also bear." He turned back to Orlynd. "I am sorry. I know you already have lost your mother and your brother. Your mother was very dear to me, and I promise you, I will forever honour her memory. I am sorry you must lose your father now, too."

"Whit?" Orlynd uttered, frantically looking towards his father.

The king turned, walked to the door of his private apartment and opened it. He looked into the eyes of Tiberius. "You are hereby exiled. Get out of my sight," he said. He then looked at Thomas and ordered, "Take Chancellor O'Brien away."

"Father!" Orlynd shouted, his eyes wide in shock. He attempted to run towards him, but was halted by the king's arm.

"Your Majesty, I beg of you!" Tiberius yelled as several guards dragged him away.

"Father!" Orlynd cried, tears rolling down his face, as he watched the scene unfold.

"Your Majesty! Your Majesty!"

CHAPTER THREE

POVEGLIA
THE KINGDOM OF ARACELLY
1238 CE

When Mierta next became aware, he found himself in a cramped room.

Where am I? he wondered as he looked around, gathering his surroundings. *What is this place?*

"You're doing great, Mrs. McKinnon. It should just be one more push and your baby will be out," stated the woman. Looking at the scene in front of him, he realised she must be a midwife.

Mother! Mierta thought, his eyes brightening, seeing his mother lying on a small bed in the centre of the room, towards the end of her delivery. He gazed around the room again. *This must be one of the sick rooms in Poveglia, the sanatorium located in the Kingdom of Aracelly. I remember Mother telling me I was born here so I would be born a warlock, and not a man.*

A man soon joined at his mother's side. He wiped a cool cloth over her brow.

Father! Oh, Mother! Please, don't ever leave us again!

A loud wailing cry came from a new-born as he was lifted into the arms of his young mother and placed near her chest. The child grabbed onto a clump of the woman's hair.

The woman called Clarinda was visually pleasing. She wore her long black hair in a twist to the side, so it hung over her shoulder and caressed her breast. Her luscious red lips left any man with the desire to kiss them, and when she looked at someone, they felt as if her mysterious green eyes were peering through to their soul.

"Mortain." She grinned. "You have a son."

That's me! I sure had a lot of hair then. Hang on, are those some blond streaks in my hair?

The court physician representing the Kingdom of Vandolay leaned in and kissed the top of the child's head. "He is beautiful, just like his mother. He has my hair, and your green eyes. What shall we name him?" He asked, his own hazel eyes betraying the pride he felt.

Clarinda studied her son for several minutes. She spoke, "His life-force is connected to this world like a river, bright yet unpredictable. He will accomplish things that shall surpass both our talents."

"Then, it is settled. We shall call him…Mierta."

As the scene began to fade into darkness, Mierta thought, *No! Don't take my mother away from me again. No! Please! Mother!*

MCKINNON ESTATE
GLENDALOW
1238 CE

"HAPPY BIRTHDAY, my boy!" Mierta heard his father's voice, before the darkness lifted and the scene came into focus.

Mortain turned in his chair towards the doorway, smiling. A quill was in one hand, while his other hand was holding down a piece of parchment.

"Thank you, Father," Mierta answered, furrowing his brow as he glanced towards the ground with uncertainty.

"What is troubling you, my boy?" Mortain questioned, gesturing for his son to come closer.

"I..." Mierta said, his heartbeat quickening.

I remember this, Mierta thought. *This just happened earlier today! I was worried how father would react.*

"I need to ask you something," Mierta said.

"Of course, my boy."

I do not understand. Why I am being shown this again? I was expecting to see something different.

"Today is my twelfth birthday," Mierta began, trying to convince himself not to be nervous.

"Why, yes, it is," replied Mortain with a smile.

"It is an important year for a boy of my age, right?"

"Yes, of course."

Mierta nodded. He looked up into his father's face. "Then I need to ask for your permission. If Mum were still alive, I am certain she would have agreed."

"I'm not sure I understand what you're asking, Mierta?" Mortain asked, curving his eyebrows.

I didn't notice father looking at me like that before. He looks so worried. I thought he wouldn't have any knowledge of the Rite of Wands.

"I request your permission to participate in the Rite of Wands. I wish to join the magical community."

There was a genuine look of fear in Mortain's eyes before the scene faded to black once more.

MCKINNON ESTATE
GLENDALOW
1260 CE

AGAIN, THE scene changed. At first, there was nothing but darkness. Slowly a landscape was unveiled.

The smell of smoke in the air lingered from a previous fire, but it didn't drown out the smell of death.

Blimey! Mierta thought, between coughs. *Where am I now? What's going on around here? It smells terrible!* Mierta gasped, seeing corpses starting to form in the scenery in front of him.

There were hundreds of them. Bodies were lying on top of each other, thrown in oversized piles like they were nothing but animals. An abandoned wheelbarrow contained more bodies.

A deadly plague called Shreya had ravaged the land of Iverna, leaving destruction in its path. The disease did not discriminate in whom it had consumed. Thousands of families had already been eliminated, and those who had been left behind were forced to bury their loved ones, only to become infected themselves.

The image of a man's brown boot appeared, and the sound of a shovel meeting fresh dirt was heard next. He lifted the dirt and tossed it aside before striking the earth again with his shovel. Leaning against it, he shifted a clump of thick brown hair out of his eyes before wiping his feverish brow with his arm.

This man probably cannot hear me, but I wish he could tell me what happened here.

Mierta watched the man examine his fingers and frown, noticing the greyish tone to his fingertips.

A wet-sounding cough escaped his lips. The ailing man appeared to be in his mid-thirties. He was wearing a long, cream-coloured tunic and black breeches. Allowing the shovel to fall to the ground while another coughing fit took hold of him, he breathed heavily; wheezing sounds could be heard when he attempted to take in a deep breath. When he was finished, he spit into the dirt and watched the blood seep in.

This man is very ill, Mierta thought. *If only there was something I could do to help him.*

The man continued to try to take in a deep breath, but it only brought on more coughs. He leaned over and waited for the fit to pass.

"I have to get back to the cellar," the man said to himself. "I need another potion. I reckon the one I made earlier should be cool by now. After, I shall rest. Yes, then I shall rest."

He sounds just like I do. Mierta thought, his eyes growing wide at the realisation. *This is from my future, which means, this man is me!*

The man turned, took a step forward and stumbled, attempting to reach out for something to keep his balance.

What's wrong with me? And where is everyone else? Is everyone dead?

"No, no, please!" the man spoke outloud, gazing up at the sky, as if someone else was conversing with him. "I'm not finished yet. I still need to conjure up a cure for the Shreya."

Shreya? I've never heard of it. Maybe father will know. I must ask him later.

The man made it back into his estate and began to walk down the stairs to the cellar.

Blimey! I look like I'm about to pass out trying to get down those stairs. It would be rather unfortunate if I fell and hurt my back.

Reaching a hand out to keep his balance, the man walked past three workbenches before he found the container holding his latest attempt at a remedy.

What is that?

The man held up the vial of liquid to his lips, drinking the concoction until he had fully consumed it. He set the empty container down on the workbench. There was a moment of fright in his eyes before his knees buckled underneath him.

What's happening? What's going on?

Mierta watched the man close his eyes and fall backward, landing on the wooden floor with a loud thud. There was nothing Mierta could do, even as the man's breathing increased then became shallower until it appeared to cease.

Get up! Get up, please! This can't be the way things end. No! Mierta screamed before all went dark.

DRACONIERA MOUNTAIN
THE KINGDOM OF ARACELLY
1238 CE

WHEN MIERTA awoke, he was back at Draconiera Mountain, in a sitting, yet somewhat slumped over position, his back pressed against the pedestal. He blinked, still trying to fully awaken from the trance.

As soon as he recognised his surroundings, he gasped and looked around. There was no evidence of blood on the ground. He then quickly examined his chest, again finding himself unscathed.

Blimey! It was a hallucination. But, what happened? Did I really die?

"Well done, young warlock," Lord Kaeto announced. "I'm sorry you had to experience such torturous dreams, but it was necessary. You have successfully been evaluated and your essence is now synced." He turned to Dragomir. "Thank you for your assistance. I'd like to speak to the boy alone. Off you go now."

Dragomir bowed, and made his way back through the doors he had first appeared from.

"You mean I passed, I succeeded? I can be part of the magical community now?" The smile on Mierta's face quickly faded as he recalled the sad expression on the dragon's face before he had lost consciousness. "You...you already knew what I was going to see," Mierta stammered. "My future...I died." He wondered if he had possibly mixed up ingredients and had somehow managed to poison himself, which resulted in his immediate death. His eyes narrowed when he looked back at Lord Kaeto. He felt his hands bending into fists, and he held the position until he could feel his fingernails digging into his skin. "Oi! My life is going to be claimed by some formidable disease?"

"Yes," Lord Kaeto replied. "I was uncertain you would accept your disheartening fate. Not many warlocks could. However, the point of the ritual isn't to show what may or may not happen to you. Rather, it's up to you to decide how you are going to react to it."

"Is there no way to prevent it?" Mierta protested. There was no way he was going to accept this destiny. "Is my fate sealed, then?"

Lord Kaeto continued. "Heed my advice, young warlock. The future you saw is only a possibility. You will be given the ability to change it."

"How?" Mierta asked.

"I suggest you start by studying your father's potion books! Don't worry, you do not need to understand magic in order to compound ingredients," Lord Kaeto stated. "And now, you must heed my warning, young warlock. I know what your heart desires. You seek power, and you are angry because a brigand murdered your mother."

At the mention of his mother, Mierta's thoughts drifted back to that horrible day, earlier this spring.

MCKINNON ESTATE
GLENDALOW
1238 CE

"SUCH A travesty..."

"The poor boy! He's too young to have lost his mother..."

Quiet voices echoed from the parlour at the McKinnon Estate. Mierta approached the top of the stairs in the entrance hall. He swiftly lowered himself against the railing when he caught the sound of his father's voice. It sounded like he had been recently crying. None of the adults were aware he was there.

"Mortain, you are certain it was Clarinda that was found in the dark alleyway two nights ago?" Mierta heard a neighbour say.

"Yes," Mortain said. "Her head had been severed, her chest had been cut open."

Mierta gasped and covered his mouth with his hands, afraid he may have given his presence away. Hot tears filled his eyes. His mother was dead, brutally murdered, and he didn't have the power to bring her back.

DRACONIERA MOUNTAIN
THE KINGDOM OF ARACELLY
1238 CE

TEARS ROLLED down Mierta's face as his thoughts returned to the present.

"You blame yourself because you believe you are weak. I understand. However, Mierta McKinnon, you are far from being a failure."

Mierta gasped at Lord Kaeto's acknowledgement, and quickly wiped the tears from his face.

The dragon continued. "You have a great destiny before you, one which you cannot even begin to comprehend. Now, on your feet. The time has come to awaken the gift your mother passed on to you. Reach out your hand and call for the wand, which will aid you in your journey!"

"Hang on, Lord Kaeto," Mierta said through nervous laughter. "You said I could summon a wand to come to me? You must be mistaken. It is impossible."

The doors from which Dragomir had originally appeared from opened with a jolt.

"Nothing is impossible, young warlock! Did you not know of your mother's talent to control things with her mind?" Lord Kaeto challenged. He didn't wait for Mierta's response before commanding, "Stand up!"

Mierta stood on shaky legs, brushed his breeches and adjusted his cloak. He could only see darkness through the doors, yet he could now feel a strong cool wind coming from an unknown source.

"Stand at a slight angle, with your right hip towards the door. Align your right leg slightly in front of you, and place your full weight on your left. Now, stretch out your right hand, turn it sideways, and raise it in front of you," Lord Kaeto instructed over the wind. "Close your eyes. Concentrate. Permit yourself to feel the energy flowing through your body, allowing you to influence the physical essence of the system without any kind of physical interaction. Now, open your eyes, and repeat after me. *Convosurí.*"

Mierta did as instructed and repeated with no inflection, "*Convosurí.*"

Lord Kaeto growled. "Put some emphasis into it, young warlock! You can't expect your wand to respond to such weak commands. You don't wish to be known as the warlock with the feeble wand, do you?"

Mierta scowled at the dragon. He could feel an energy brewing inside his body from an unknown source. Water crashed against rocks like the beginning of a severe thunderstorm, and Mierta's eyes transformed into the shape of a snake's.

Mierta refocused on the doors, and spoke with a commanding voice, "*Convosurí!*"

The ground shook under his feet, and an ebony wooden wand with a bloodstone crystal connected at the shaft flew out of the darkness.

Each wand was as unique as its bearer, bringing its own abilities and enhancements due to the crystal it carried. Some wands brought prosperity, some brought healing abilities, some brought clarity, and some brought on dreams. No two wands were designed the same, and each was synced to a witch or warlock's life-force.

Mierta took ahold of the wand in his hand and stared at it. His wand brought on strength, inner courage and vitality. Slowly, he closed his eyes, feeling his body becoming instantly rewarded by his new wand's powers.

CHAPTER FOUR

COINNEACH CASTLE
THE KINGDOM OF VANDOLAY
1238 CE

F ather," uttered Orlynd, staring at the empty hallway where his
father once stood. A deep sadness grew in the pit of his stomach.
He calmed himself, overcoming the shock of the day's events.

Ah'm never going tae see him again, concluded Orlynd.

"Orlynd," Francis said, startling the warlock from his thoughts.

Francis held his hand out towards the direction of the dining
room. "Please, follow me. I wish to speak more privately." Orlynd
watched Francis share a warning glance with Thomas before read-
dressing him. "I assure you, young warlock, we will be permitted to
interact without further interruptions," he finished.

Orlynd hesitated, watching Thomas lower his head in shame and
close the door behind them. He took in a deep breath and followed
the king.

As they entered the room, Orlynd was overcome by the sight before him. In the centre of the room was a large table covered in a white lace tablecloth. There were ten place settings of the finest plates Orlynd had ever seen. The silver candleholders in the centre of the table gleamed in the light and held tall, thin, white candles just waiting to be lit.

On the right wall, a portrait of the king took up most of the space allowed. Underneath the portrait was a smaller table, covered with a matching lace tablecloth, upon which large covered platters sat. Orlynd was certain they would soon hold the most delectable meats found in the entire kingdom.

At the far end was an elegant fireplace that could warm the entire room against even the coldest weather. The floor he stood on was covered with a thick, ornately decorated rug, which stretched to the farthest corners of the room. Orlynd came back to himself and realised he had stopped, frozen, just inside the doorway.

"Fear not. Please, be seated. You may speak freely." Francis walked over to a large pitcher and picked up a silver goblet from the table. "May I offer you some mead? My servants locate the finest mead available in all of Iverna," he stated, pouring himself a drink.

"Thank yis, Yir Grace," Orlynd answered, afraid of offending the king if he refused.

Francis took a large gulp before setting his goblet down on the table. He then poured a cup for Orlynd. "How old are you, Orlynd?"

"Sixteen, Yir Grace," Orlynd answered, raising the goblet to his lips to take a sip. He was surprised by the flavour of the gorse flower mead, which finished with a sweet taste of honey, coconut and vanilla, and how easily it travelled down his throat.

"Sixteen, a fine age," Francis said, taking a seat. "Tell me, Orlynd. What interests you? Do you enjoy reading?" The king raised his goblet to his lips.

"Aye, Yir Grace. Ah enjoy reading scrolls n manuscripts."

Francis's eyes sparkled as he raised his eyebrows. "Is that so?" he responded, smiling. "Our kingdom contains some of the finest librar- ies. I am confident you would have made a good scholar." His gaze turned to the table and his expression changed from friendly to con- templative. He took another sip of his mead before setting it down in front of him.

"Is something wrong, Yir Grace?" Orlynd asked.

Francis cleared his throat. "I have decided tomorrow morning you will begin lessons in proper etiquette. The education you will receive shall be suited for a royal. You will be granted access to my libraries, which will assist you in your studies on the customs and history of the kingdom. You will be expected to have this knowledge when you accompany me or the prince. Have you had the honour of meeting my son? He is just a few years younger than you."

"Nae, Yir Grace."

"Naught to fear. There shall be plenty of time for you to become acquainted. You shall be joining him during his language lessons. He is currently composing a love poem in French to impress the Lady Anya from Glendalow. She has been promised to my son and will someday be his queen."

"How very thoughtful ay His Grace," Orlynd responded.

"I am glad you approve. Now, that's enough socialising for today. I must finish preparing for the celebration of my son's fourteenth birthday. I do expect you to attend the festivities. It shall begin with an amazing jousting tournament where my son, Déor, shall challenge the winning competitor," he grinned egoistically. He then stopped smiling. "It is important my son wins to prove the crown is strong. You shall be permitted to explore the castle halls and the grounds at your leisure. This is your home now, and there is no better time than the present to start getting yourself familiar with it. The navigation can be challenging. You will find the castle and its various buildings contain over one hundred rooms! You may leave me now."

"Aye, Sire," Orlynd answered, standing up from his chair quickly. He abruptly stopped and turned towards the king.

"What is it?" Francis asked, leaning forward, getting annoyed.

"Ah'm sorry, Yir Grace, but Ah dinnae know how tae find my room."

"Of course you don't," The king said, gesturing with his hand before shouting, "Thomas!"

"Yes, Your Grace," Thomas said, bowing, after reentering the room.

"Please accompany Orlynd to his room. I do not wish for him to get lost, understand?"

"Yes, Sire," Thomas said, nodding. He paused. "And where would that be exactly, Your Grace?"

Francis thought for a moment, contemplating where best to house the boy without problems arising in the castle due to the O'Brien name. "There is an empty cottage just outside the gate at the edge of the village, is there not?"

"Yes, Your Grace," Thomas replied.

"Then it is settled. It shall now belong to Orlynd," Francis said, turning to the warlock. "Understand, it is not much, but it shall provide you a roof over your head until better arrangements can be made."

"Aye, Yir Grace. Thank yis, Yir Grace."

"Now, please leave me."

They bowed to the king before taking their leave.

Once the king was alone, he raised his hands and rubbed them down his face, blowing air slowly out through pursed lips, pondering whether he had made the correct decision regarding Tiberius.

MCKINNON ESTATE
GLENDALOW
1238 CE

"MIERTA? ARE you all right?" Mortain asked, approaching the parlour. "You have not said a word since we returned from your Rite of Wands." Mortain, a man of average height, was dressed in the custom of his profession, his long, blue tunic all but covering the red undergarments he wore.

"I'm fine, Father," Mierta said, staring towards the empty fireplace. He was seated at a cherrywood table staring at the wall. A full cup of tea, which had been placed on the table in front of him, had long since gone cold. The top crust of his pot pie had been cut away and set aside, and his wand was lying next to it.

"You are not fine," Mortain said, removing his black hat and running his fingers through his medium-length brown hair. He approached the table. "Son, you have barely touched your dinner. Please, tell me what is bothering you."

When his son didn't reply, Mortain walked to the opposite side of the table and glanced him over with concern. His son's face had gone pale. Droplets of cold sweat had already soaked his sideburns. Mortain went to his son's side and laid a cool hand over Mierta's brow, becoming alarmed. "My dear boy, what is wrong? Your skin is clammy, yet your body is freezing." He turned and shouted towards the kitchen, "Armand!"

"Monsieur McKinnon?" the servant Armand questioned from the parlour entrance, upon hearing Mortain's voice. He was a tall young man in his late teens. His long, curly, black hair had been tied back at the base of his neck. A short well-trimmed beard covered his strong jaw line, and his upper lip was covered by a thin moustache under a long beak-like nose. His fiery brown eyes betrayed his weary countenance.

"Armand," Mortain said, glancing over and struggling to hide his worry. He lowered his hand from Mierta's brow and took a hold of his son's hand, pretending to check his pulse. "Please set a fire in the fireplace. My son is not well, and I must tend to him. Then, please fetch me milk of the poppy, and bring it to Mierta's room."

"Oui, Monsieur," Armand answered, starting a small fire in the grate.

Mortain waited till the servant had left before furrowing his eyebrows and turning his attention back to his son. "Mierta? Please, son, speak to me. I know I have not always been the best confidant. Your mum was much better at that, but I wish to help you."

"You cannot," Mierta answered, a bit coldly.

Mortain gazed into Mierta's eyes, becoming further disturbed when a single tear fell from Mierta's right eye. Frustrated, he wiped his hand over his face and down his prominent chin wishing Clarinda were still alive. She had had the most impressive ability to help those in need, and Mortain at that very moment needed her assistance desperately. However, she was not there, and Mortain had no choice but to aid their son through whatever was ailing him. "Please, my son. Let me try!" He was beginning to feel helpless.

Mierta looked up into his father's face, furrowing his forehead, contemplating his situation. He couldn't tell his father. Discussion of his Rite of Wands was forbidden, even though he desperately needed his father's advice at the moment. He had very little knowledge about compounding chemicals, and though it was never said, it was expected of him to follow in his father's footsteps, for that was what all fathers wished of their eldest child; it saved them from having to pay a stranger for their child's apprenticeship and worry about his well-being. Nonetheless, Mierta was afraid. What if he failed or disappointed his father? "I'm sorry," Mierta's voice cracked. "I…cannot explain."

Mortain took a deep breath. "You have been thinking about your Rite of Wands ceremony, right, my boy?" he asked, continuing to comfort his son.

"Yes," Mierta uttered, unable to get the scenes out of his mind.

Mortain brushed his hand down Mierta's arm, feeling is son's body tremble. "Oh, my poor boy. I understand. It is a burden only you must bear, but you must remember that it is over now."

"Is it?" Mierta said with doubt in his heart, not expecting a response. His mum would have understood. She was a witch and had gone through the Rite of Wands herself, but his father…he was just a man. "Father?" Mierta asked.

"Yes, my boy?"

"When I told you I wanted to participate in the Rite of Wands, you looked scared. I want to know why."

Mortain nervously laughed it off. "I apologise if I looked that way, my boy. That was not my intention. I was just surprised!"

"I see." Mierta looked down at the cold cup of tea, unable to look his father in the eye. He mumbled to the ground, "Do you suppose the reason the Rite of Wands is not to be discussed is because people have gone mad?" The question was hypothetical. Again, he didn't expect Mortain to have the answer. He just wanted his father to listen.

"I suppose anything is possible, my son," Mortain responded, quickly becoming uncomfortable by the direction of the conversation.

"I am frightened. I fear I will not be able to do what was asked of me."

"Mierta, look at me," his father instructed.

Mierta obeyed, crinkling his brow.

Mortain took his son's hands into his. "Whatever it was that you think was asked of you, I am confident you will succeed. Pray with me, my boy. Hand your troubles over to our good Lord. You are not alone. Let us pray for your soul."

Mierta watched his father close his eyes and prepare to pray. He sighed and looked away. He didn't understand why his father even bothered to pray. It seemed like nothing but a waste of breath. What had prayer ever done for their family? It hadn't saved his mother, and if what the Rite of Wands had shown him was true, it wouldn't save him from the upcoming plague.

"Lord, hear our prayer. Bless my son, Mierta. Keep him safe from Satan's will. Heal my boy's tormented soul, and protect him when he feels weak. May your mighty will be done. Amen."

Mortain opened his eyes and smiled at his son. Mierta returned a half smile. "Thank you, Father," Mierta answered, though Mortain could see the uncertainty in his face.

"Pleasure, my dear boy," Mortain said, squeezing his hands and standing back up.

"Father?" Mierta asked, nervously.

"Yes?"

"What do you suppose happens if someone chooses not to do what the Rite of Wands shows you to do? Do you think that person or those people might get in trouble?"

"I have no idea, my boy."

"Didn't Mum ever discuss the Rite of Wands with you? I mean, you told me she always wanted me to be a warlock. That's why I decided to go through the test."

"I'm not sure what you are asking, Mierta?"

"Never mind," Mierta sighed, feeling like a fool. His father was just an ordinary man; he could never understand the torment Mierta was feeling inside.

I suggest you start by studying your father's potion books, Mierta recalled Lord Kaeto stating.

"S…suppose what the Rite of Wands warned turned out to be true? What if it had the power to show you what you were supposed to do or who you were supposed to be?" Mierta said. He looked up at his father, his eyes begging for an explanation.

"I'm afraid I do not have the answers you seek, my son," Mortain replied, frowning. He wished he could comfort his son and assure Mierta what he was feeling was valid. However, he couldn't reveal the truth about his past. He couldn't tell him he was also a warlock, or at least used to be. Not yet.

"May I make a request?" Mierta questioned.

"And what may that be, my boy?"

"You cannot always be here for me and Lochlann," Mierta began, looking away. "I know this. It would be selfish to think otherwise."

He glanced back at his father. "You have patients in the Kingdom of Vandolay needing your care, and we have Armand. However, in your absence, I promise to look after Lochlann, as an older brother should. Please, I beg of you, teach me what you do."

"I do not understand what you mean, Mierta," Mortain answered.

"I request an apprenticeship," Mierta replied with urgency in his voice. "I want to help people. I want to be a physician like you."

Mortain was touched by the request. "How very courageous of you, my son, but that will have to wait until you are finished with your formal schooling, and, if I recall correctly, when I had last travelled with you to the Kingdom of Vandolay, you showed little interest in my doings."

"That's because you didn't need to use any potions. I wish to learn how to brew medicines," Mierta countered.

"Is that so? Then, if I may suggest, the profession you desire to study is apothecary, my boy. I'm afraid there are no apothecaries in Glendalow; however, when you are of the proper age of fourteen, I can teach you a little bit about herbs and how to weave chemicals together, and if you still show interest, I shall introduce you to a guild in Edesia."

"But, Father, I must start learning now. I cannot wait till I'm fifteen for a perfect apprenticeship," Mierta pleaded.

"Mierta, there is far more to apothecary than playing around with compounds! Why the rush? You will have to spend many hours studying diseases, medications, and even how to perform minor surgeries. And, you will have to pass an examination through the guild," Mortain responded.

"I know about your elixir book of recipes!" Mierta blurted out, unable to hide his irritation.

"My...what?" Mortain asked, stunned.

"You know what I'm talking about," Mierta answered. "You cannot hide the truth from me, Father. I know you once studied apothecary, too."

Mortain snorted. "It is no secret, my son. In order to become a court physician, one must understand the basic principles of compounding."

"Then, you will permit me access to your book," Mierta insisted.

"Blimey! I appreciate your interest, Mierta," Mortain got up and turned his body away, pausing. He furrowed his eyebrows. "However, I do not know where it is."

"Why are you lying to me? What is in the book you do not wish me to see?"

Mortain turned back and half smiled. "Forgive me. It's not that I do not desire you to have access to it, Mierta. You are my son. It's just…" He sighed. "When you are older you will understand. The life of an Apothecarist is not simply mixing herbs and potions."

"I do not wish for simple. I understand what I must do," Mierta responded, his voice breaking.

"Enough discussion for today. I asked Armand to fetch some milk of the poppy. It will help you sleep. You need to rest. It has been a long day."

"You do not understand," Mierta said, standing up. "You cannot possibly understand what I know, what I have seen! Every moment I am delayed costs me in ways you will never understand."

"You are right, my son," Mortain interrupted, regretfully. "I cannot understand how important this is to you. However, I can confirm you have always been wiser than your age. Most adults could not conjure up such a persuasive argument. I realise now I was wrong to lie to you. I must accept I cannot prevent you from the life you are destined for. I should know better than anyone, you cannot escape your fate."

"What do you mean? Did something happen to you?" Mierta asked, his eyes wide with curiosity and confusion.

"Never mind, Mierta. One day I shall tell you everything." He gazed at his son. Mierta's mouth parted as if to protest.

"Until then, forget I even said anything. It is for the best." He sighed again, seeing the disappointment in Mierta's face. "If you are still insistent on beginning to master the technique of compounding, I reckon the book you seek is still down in the cellar somewhere. The cellar has not been used in decades; it is a bit old-fashioned. That's the last place I recall using it. It was a long time ago, you see. I was merely a teenager myself. It's probably covered in cobwebs now and God knows what else. If the book is salvable, the recipes will be simple enough to comprehend. Remain here. I shall return in a moment." When he returned he held out a key to his son. "I reckon you will need this."

Mierta's eyes lit up.

"I dare say I have had this key in my possession hidden away in a dresser drawer for the longest time. It is yours now. I know it is pointless for me to try to stop you, but please, do be careful when you go looking for the book. The cellar is very dark and unorganised. There are many things you should not touch."

Mierta smiled. "I promise to be careful. Thank you, Father."

Mortain nodded. "Right. Now, pick up your wand from the table and follow me. Armand will be here with your poppy milk shortly. It is past your bedtime, after all. Remember, a wand can be a warlock's lifeline. Never let it out of your sight," Mortain announced, gesturing for Mierta to follow. "Tomorrow morning, I begin my journey to the Kingdom of Vandolay. The king has prearranged a commemoration of the prince's birthday in the park of Coinneach Castle. The king would certainly have my head if I dared to miss the celebration."

CHAPTER FIVE

TARLOCH CASTLE
GLENDALOW
1238 CE

A wooden door creaked as it slowly opened, revealing a single ray of light leaking into the cell through a small crevice in the rocky wall. The light from the hallway helped create a shadow of the Hand of the King's knee-high boots, which were made of the finest dark leather and covered most of his silvery undertunic.

He listened for the rattling sound of the prisoner's chains.

The prisoner, a frail woman wearing a grey, torn set of rags, sat against the wall with her legs pulled up against her chest. Her filthy brown hair, long enough to reach her toes, hid the woman's face, protecting her eyes from the light.

"Why do you continue to live on? There is nothing left in this world for you," he hissed.

"I request to see Anya," the woman said.

Ciarán laughed, brushing his blond hair that hung just below his shoulders behind him. He was dressed in a forest green tunic bearing the sigil of his house. A golden belt, from which hung a long sword, was cinched around his waist.

"And why should you desire to see her?"

"I am her mother. That permits me to see her," she uttered.

"Is that so?" Ciarán smirked. "No one knows you are here, Katrina. It is a shame you have withered away into a shell of what you once were, and yet, here you remain, continuing to live like a flea feeding off a host. This is not how it had to be for you; however, you made that choice when you chose to deceive me."

"I did what I had to do to make your line stronger! Now, I demand to see our daughter!" Katrina snapped.

"If you haven't already figured it out, allow me to inform you Anya does not wish to see you," Ciarán answered coldly. "You no longer exist. In fact, she has no knowledge you've ever been a prisoner here, wasting away these six long years. She was notified you died from grief after losing our son. Even if she knew the truth, she would not wish to see you. There is no love left in her heart for you. But have no fear. I have continued to look after her as a father should. Soon, she shall be given her chance to rightfully claim what is hers when the royal line of O'Connor in the Kingdom of Vandolay is no more. My plan is already being implemented."

COINNEACH CASTLE
THE KINGDOM OF VANDOLAY
1238 CE

"YOU WISHED to see me, Father?" Déor asked, after entering his father's private apartment and stepping into the dining area. He bowed before his father and kissed the top of his ring.

"Aye," Francis said. "There is an important matter that I wish to discuss. Please, be seated."

With a mix of concern and curiosity, Déor did as instructed.

"Tell me, how go the preparations for the jousting tournament?" the king asked.

"Is that why you wanted an audience?" Déor inquired.

"Nay," Francis said, half smiling. He sighed. "I suppose you will discover soon enough. I have accepted a new soothsayer."

Déor sat up straight in his chair. "But, Father, you just got rid of the last one. What in blazes made you think we needed another one so soon? What does this soothsayer have to offer us?"

"He's not just any soothsayer. He's the son of Tiberius O'Brien."

"An O'Brien," Déor said, standing up from his chair. "For God's sake, have you gone mad? You have purposefully put the crown in danger!"

"You forget your place! Last I checked, I was King, not you." Francis said, his anger rising. "I believe he will be useful to us. His father mentioned his eyes will change and appear to have fragments of flames when he uses his gift. This is how I will know if he is telling the truth. Orlynd has already predicted the Kingdom of Aracelly means to interfere with the crown, which is why you must win the tournament. It is important to demonstrate the crown is strong, even if you may be feeling otherwise. I promise you will be greatly rewarded."

MCKINNON ESTATE
GLENDALOW
1260 CE

AN INTENSE wind blew against Mierta's face, sending smoke through the air. It carried an aroma of dirt and faeces, followed by the suffocating stench of burning flesh. Mierta held out a hand to see through the haze as the scene unfolded. He was alone; the land he was standing on, once covered with grass, was now barren or burned out.

A large pile of bodies slowly became clear. Hundreds of corpses lay piled on top of each other, some still wearing clothes, while only the body parts of others remained. He watched a bird of prey peck at one of the dead, while flies buzzed about.

His thoughts became distracted when he recognised the man whom he believed was a representation of an older version of himself, appearing just a few feet in front of him, digging a large hole into the ground.

Hang on. I have been here before. This was in my Rite of Wands ceremony and that's...me. What am I doing back here? Mierta thought to himself, crinkling his brow and turning his attention to his older self.

"Um. Hello?" he said with some hesitation.

The man continued to dig into the ground. He lifted his shovel and threw dirt in Mierta's direction, practically hitting him.

"Oi, watch where you're throwing that!" Mierta scolded. He watched the man continue digging. Mierta shrugged his shoulders. "I guess he cannot hear me," he realised, but his thoughts were interrupted by the now familiar sound of his older self—coughing. He composed himself and directed his attention back to the scene before him.

Maybe I'm supposed to see something I didn't before? Mierta thought, slowly approaching his older self, just in time to see him spit blood onto the ground.

Mierta curved his eyebrows and looked around again. The bodies...they had all died from a disease. Everyone was dead.

"No, no, no, this cannot happen," Mierta cried, dropping to his knees, panic starting to set in as he placed his hands over the sides of his face. He lowered his head and shouted, "This isn't real!"

The scene rapidly spun and abruptly came to a stop with the sound of a door slamming. Mierta opened his eyes, looked up, and lowered his hands. He was no longer outside. Now, he was inside some place dark and musty. He could feel the wood under his knees and hear the sound of something being stirred. Again, the man was there, pouring whatever concoction he had just mixed into a small culture tub.

Mierta stood up quickly, knowing what was going to happen next. "No, you daft idiot! Don't drink it! It will kill you!" Mierta shouted, watching the man pick up the potion and raise it to his lips. "NO!" Mierta screamed, racing towards him, leaping up and knocking it out of his hands, but not before he had finished drinking it.

The man gazed down and parted his mouth, seeing what remained of the tube shattered in pieces at his feet. He slowly looked up and crinkled his brow, finding himself staring into the eyes of his younger self.

Mierta gasped, realising he had not only been too late, but the man appeared to be able to see him now.

This is impossible. I can't be in two places at the same time! This cannot be real. Mother, please help me!

The man reached out a hand, as if questioning whether what he was experiencing was a hallucination or not. He reached up to pinch his cheek, regretting the decision right away.

He gazed at Mierta with a disturbed expression on his face. "You are not supposed to be here," he said.

Mierta gazed back at him with the same expression.

This could not be real! This could not possibly be real!

The man took one step forward towards him when his knees buckled, and his body fell backward meeting the cherrywood floor with a loud thud.

Mierta watched the man's breathing quicken before growing shallower and then ceasing.

"No!" he heard himself scream. He was uncertain if it was him or someone else.

MCKINNON ESTATE
GLENDALOW
1238 CE

"MUM!"

Mierta startled awake, quickly sitting up in bed. He breathed in and out rapidly, trying to calm his racing heart as he looked about the room. Everything was quiet. He stood up on his bed and peered out the window. There was nothing to be seen but darkness. He barely could make out the waves crashing against the rocks coming from the bottom of the hill.

It's still night out, he thought. The sun hadn't even attempted to rise yet.

Mierta sat back down on the bed and pulled the covers closer to his body as he trembled.

"What is wrong with me?" he thought to himself, tears starting to fall down his face. *"Mother...I'm afraid. I'm so very afraid."*

ORLYND'S COTTAGE
THE KINGDOM OF VANDOLAY
1238 CE

ORLYND STIRRED to what sounded like a soft, wet thump against the front door of his cottage. He didn't fully wake until he heard the sound again.

Wit is that sound? He wondered, pulling back his blanket.

He looked down, realising he had slept in his clothes from the day before, after crying himself to sleep. Slowly, he sat up, brushed his hands over his face, and allowed his legs to dangle over the edge of the bed. He gazed around the cottage. It wasn't much for living arrangements, but at the same time, he was grateful to have a roof over his head. It was simple in design. A single room with a chest of drawers made of a rough wood in one corner and a desk and chair, seemingly made from the same tree, were positioned in the middle of the room. The bed on which he slept was nothing more than a wood frame with a straw-stuffed sack for a mattress. The stove, which was used for warmth as much as cooking, stood opposite of the only door.

He would have to prove his loyalty before he could be rewarded with anything more than plain comforts.

Next, he heard what sounded like something breaking against the door.

Whit is going oan? he wondered, deciding to investigate the noise.

He stood up and slowly made his way to the front door. Opening it, he saw two young boys standing in the street. One had his hand raised, ready to release another egg at Orlynd's door.

"Oi! Whit ur yis doing?" Orlynd called out.

Realising they had been caught, the boys shrieked, dropped the remains of rotten vegetables, and ran off.

Looking down Orlynd discovered broken egg shells among various smashed vegetables. Confused and unsure of what was happening, Orlynd absentmindedly cleaned up the mess and retreated into the cottage.

CHAPTER SIX

COINNEACH CASTLE
THE KINGDOM OF VANDOLAY
1238 CE

O rlynd had wandered around aimlessly, not sure where he had been or where he was going. He turned a corner and found himself in an impossibly long corridor, which seemed to go on for an eternity.

The walls were painted a royal blue colour, the doors and windows were framed by ornately carved wood, painted gold, and the cross beams at the ceiling contained gilded carvings of different animal and bird heads.

Perhaps these are representations ay the animals that can be found in the kingdom, Orlynd guessed.

Lining the walls were what appeared to be at least two to three hundred paintings by various artists. The pictures Orlynd saw included landscapes, along with ones of many generations of the royal family, as well as some of the members of the court.

Orlynd stopped abruptly and turned, noticing one of the paintings on the wall was a depiction of his father wearing his full religious garments, during a time when the O'Brien name was still honourable.

He breathed out a slow breath between his lips and stared up at his father's image. Orlynd's gaze was so intense, it was as if he was attempting to communicate telepathically to the portrait. He pulled his hands together under his robe and raised them up to his waist.

Everyone Ah've ever loved has left me, even yis. How am Ah tae make yis proud? How can Ah dae this when Ah know Ah will never see yis again? Ah'm all alone, Orlynd thought.

"Who are you?" a demanding voice behind Orlynd said. He turned to see a young man, slightly shorter, no older than his early teens, standing about a foot behind him. The teenage boy had piercing baby blue eyes and long curly brown hair, which was tied back in a braid. He was wearing a maize coloured tunic with black accents and a black belt wrapped around him, with a cream coloured silk shirt underneath, and black boots.

Orlynd bowed, realising the boy could be no one other than the king's son.

"Ma apologises, Yir Grace. Ah dinnae hear yis approach," Orlynd stammered.

The prince advanced, so he could inspect the painting that had captured Orlynd's attention. He stopped next to the warlock, looked up at the painting and then gazed back at Orlynd, displeased. "Enlighten me. What do you find so interesting about this portrait?"

"Ah...err," Orlynd muttered, contemplating how to answer the question.

The prince narrowed his eyes. "Are you refusing to answer my question?"

"Nae, Yir Grace," Orlynd quickly responded.

Déor eyed Orlynd, tilting his head slightly. "I don't believe I recall seeing your face in my father's court before. What is your name and what house do you belong to?"

"Orlynd," the warlock answered, growing intimated by the prince's presence. He watched the prince circle him.

"Orlynd," Déor said, eyeing him suspiciously. He stopped to glance back at the painting before turning back to the warlock. "Of course! You must be the warlock from Aracelly my father informed me about." He turned back to the portrait before continuing. "And that painting is a representation of your father," he confirmed, looking over the warlock with a bit of a smug grin. "My, you're pretty skinny. Do you even have anything under your robe?"

Orlynd shooed the prince's hand away.

Déor chuckled, amused, before his expression changed over to a scowl. "Show me your wand, warlock."

Orlynd stared at him in defiance.

"I said," Déor said more firmly, "show me your wand."

Orlynd did as he was told, pulling out his wand from a pocket of his breeches. He held it out in front of him nervously.

The prince shrugged his shoulders. "Pity. It looks pretty plain to me. I've never seen a wand as pathetic looking as yours."

"It's not pathetic!" Orlynd hissed. "Ma wand is designed tae bring enlightenment, n' help clarify the true intentions ay people around me."

"Is that so?" Déor challenged. "Tell me then, what am I thinking right now?"

"Ah cannae," Orlynd said, putting his wand away.

"You cannot, or you will not?" Déor mocked, circling around the warlock again, stopping abruptly when he was face-to-face with Orlynd. "So, you're really expecting me to believe you're my father's new soothsayer?"

"Ah am," Orlynd said, growing uneasy.

"Well," Déor laughed. "Go on then. Tell me my future, warlock."

Orlynd stared at him with bewilderment.

Déor stared at him coldly. "You think you can disobey me? I am the crown prince. I told you to tell me my future! I command you to!"

Orlynd's mind raced to come up with an explanation why he could not fulfil the prince's request. Déor would never understand he had just recently acquired the ability and could not manipulate it to his will.

"Fool," Déor said, shaking his head. "I was only jesting. Seriously, you cannot do it, can you? Thought so. You're as worthless as the last man who claimed to be a soothsayer. It confirms my suspicions that my father only selected you out of pity. There are whispers that he is going mad. I cannot deny the claim myself. Why, if I had been King, I would have burned your father at the stake."

"Dinnae speak ill ay ma father!" Orlynd answered angrily, raising a fist.

"Or what? Are you going to hit me, warlock? Or, maybe threaten to turn me into a frog!" Déor grinned, amused. "I dare you to." His expression quickly changed to disgust. "Once word spreads of your incompetence, you will be made the laughingstock of the kingdom. You are no use to the king nor to me. It would be better if you were gone sooner than later."

He turned his attention to one of servants hurrying the hallway. "You there," he stated, pointing. He then pointed to the painting of Orlynd's father. "Take this portrait down and get it out of my sight!"

He looked back to Orlynd and smirked. He said maliciously, "You will notice that kind of filth is unwelcome here. It is just a matter of time before you are unwanted, too. Better watch your head, warlock!"

CHAPTER SEVEN

COINNEACH CASTLE
THE KINGDOM OF VANDOLAY
1238 CE

All hail His Royal Majesty, Francis, King of Vandolay," the herald announced, one mid-August afternoon. When the king and his new advisor approached the stairs to the Royal Box, the crowd erupted in applause, which drowned out the questioning whispers.

As they began their climb up the stairs, the king waved to the crowd and looked out over the field. The stands had been decorated with green and white banners of the royal family crest and were filled with lords and ladies from various houses in the kingdom. Francis was pleased to see the wooden barrier, which stretched most of the length of the field, had been repaired after an unfortunate incident during the previous jousting festivities.

Looking to either end of the barrier, the king smiled when he saw several tents set up, each one carrying the colours and sigils of the different houses the knights were representing. His eyes lingered briefly on the tent bearing his own sigil—a green shield with a golden split-tailed lion leaning against a great helm with a golden visor and magnificent green and gold feathers. His heart warmed, reminding him of his love for his son, his only heir, who was preparing himself for the one-on-one challenge.

This was extra special for the royal family because today the king would pass on a family heirloom, a pendant said to have been created by a warlock from the Kingdom of Aracelly, in order to protect the royal line from elimination. The king himself had never seen the charm do any magic, so there was doubt in his mind of the pendant's origin or whether any part of the story he had been told as a child was true; however, he hoped once he placed it around his son's neck, these doubts would be put to rest.

The king took his place in the farthest seat on the right while Orlynd hesitated. He wondered why there were three chairs when only the king was seated. Before Orlynd could question, the king interrupted his thoughts.

"You shall stand beside me. The other seats are for the Lord High Steward, and his daughter, Lady Anya, who is betrothed to my son," Francis stated, turning his head, hearing a carriage approach. "And what splendid timing. Their carriage arrives."

Orlynd turned around and slipped his arms inside the sleeves of his robe, while he took his place next to the king's chair. He looked up to see a magnificent carriage approaching the fairgrounds. It was shaped like a shield with a stylised crown on top and was covered in gold leaf. There were three windows through which the occupants could see the passing countryside or, more importantly, through which the people could see them. The panels below the windows were a forest green, the official colour of the steward.

The door of the carriage promptly opened, and servants waited for their appearance. First, stepped out the steward, known to the people of Vandolay as the Hand of the King and the overseer of court trials. He reached behind him for his daughter, who had cautiously placed her hand on the side of the carriage. Her festive dress equally caught the attention of women and men with its flashy royal blue and gold colouring with golden lacing.

"Herald!" Francis commanded, startling the herald who had become enchanted by Lady Anya's beauty.

"All hail, Lord High Steward Ciarán Hrodulf, and his daughter, Lady Anya of Glendalow!" yelled the herald promptly.

Anya was a beautiful, intelligent, medium-sized young woman, the same age as the crowned prince. She had a perfect, light complexion, when not hidden by enormous amounts of makeup, piercing hazel eyes, and well-developed breasts. Her long blonde hair was tied up in a bun while wavy strands lay loose on each side of her face.

Francis smiled, watching Orlynd's facial expressions closely, believing the warlock was becoming charmed. "Lady Anya is very pleasing to the eye, is she not?"

"Aye," Orlynd replied, distracted, not by the Anya's beauty, but by a warning he felt in his heart. Something did not feel right. He continued to stare at them as they made their way towards the Royal Box.

"She comes to us from Glendalow," Francis said, nodding in the direction of Anya. "Glendalow is one of the former kingdoms in Iverna, now a conquered territory of Vandolay. She resides with her father, who serves as my hand, at Tarloch Castle, where all of our rather difficult prisoners are sent. She shall one day be your queen, and with utmost certainty, will lead this kingdom to greatness. If she were not already betrothed to my son, I would be happy to claim her."

Anya looked up, catching Orlynd and the king staring at her. At that moment, Orlynd saw a vision of the royal goblet placed on a table. A small amount of clear liquid was being added to the ale, which was already in it.

The royal goblet. Someone means tae dae His Grace harm, Orlynd concluded.

Francis leaned in, startling Orlynd. He laughed, seeing a blush starting to form over Orlynd's cheeks, before continuing. "She has grown into quite the woman. She knows what she wants and how to get it. These people will love her just as I do," Francis teased before turning his attention back to his guests.

"Yer Grace, Ah must inform yis ay something," Orlynd began anxiously, only to be ignored.

"Lord High Steward!" Francis greeted the noble party. "I am honoured with your presence. I have specifically arranged these chairs for the duration of the tournament."

"Thank you, Your Grace," the steward replied after bowing. "There is no need to be so benevolent. The honour is ours. May it please Your Majesty to present to you my daughter, Anya. If I recall correctly it has been several years since she has seen Your Highness, has it not?"

"Aye, it has," replied Francis, his eyes twinkling. He gazed at Anya. "Please, approach my lady."

"Your Grace," Anya responded with a half-smile, her lips tucked in slightly. She curtsied and bent her body forward, keeping her eyes locked on the king. In doing so, she exposed the top of her cleavage, yet concealed the vial of clear liquid between the cleft of her breasts.

"Your beauty is ravishing, my lady. You will make a satisfying wife for my son," the king said, charmed.

"Thank you, Your Grace," she answered, with a smile.

"Please, allow me to introduce you both to my new advisor from the Kingdom of Aracelly, the warlock, Orlynd. He is the son of Celeste, my former advisor."

"Lord Steward, milady," Orlynd bowed, growing more uneasy. There was something very wrong with these two. It felt as if darkness filled their hearts, but he could not figure out why.

The steward and his daughter nodded back.

"Now, it will please me to have you be more present in this kingdom," the king interjected. "Would you like that, Lady Anya?"

"Yes, Your Grace," she answered with a smile.

Orlynd felt further unease. Her smile came too quickly and was not matched in her eyes.

"Then it shall be! Please, take a seat beside me. I must address my subjects about the tournament in my son's honour."

Francis stood from his chair to address the crowd. When the cheers and applause subsided, he proceeded. "Good people of the realm, and those from visiting lands, I thank you for joining me for today's festivities. Today marks the day my son, the crown prince, becomes the rightful age to marry, and therefore a special entertainment has been arranged for his guests, in which the best knights of the realm shall joust till all save one have been disqualified. By the crown's tradition, my son shall challenge this knight in order to earn his place as champion! May the best knight or royal prevail! Afterward, please join us for dining and dancing in the banquet hall. Lord High Steward, if you would please do the honours," he said, gesturing to the steward.

The Lord High Steward stood from his chair and promptly announced, "Let the tournament begin!"

An eruption of cheering filled the stands as the first two knights took their positions. The first to face the king's guard was Antonio. He came from a very noble family and was the son of a prominent general. His arrogance was unfathomable, and most of the knights whose names were on the list had grown tired of his endless boasting.

Aindrias, the king's guard, stared Antonio down. Losing wasn't an option for he could not see himself handling the embarrassment. He lowered his helmet and commanded his horse to charge down the barrier towards his opponent. Antonio's lance was knocked out of his hands, while Aindrias's lance shattered after making contact between the saddle and helm.

"Three points for Aindrias!" the herald announced.

"I expect that shall not be the last lance to break today," Francis smirked.

"Forgive me, Yir Grace," Orlynd said while the knights prepared for their next pass. "Is nae thir something less dangerous tae celebrate the prince's coming ay age?"

"And what would you consider is appropriate?" Francis challenged.

"Ah dinnae know, Yir Grace," Orlynd answered.

"Let me remind you, yesterday you were nothing more than the boy of a banished chancellor. Be grateful your mother was honourable."

The Lord High Steward cleared his throat while Anya glanced over to the warlock, a sly smile escaping her lips.

Orlynd felt heat rise to his cheeks again.

"With all due respect, Your Grace, the warlock is only concerned about your son's continued health and good fortune," the steward commented.

"My son is not some mandrake mymmerkin, Steward!" Francis snapped.

"Good gracious, he is not. I'm sure the warlock meant no offense," Ciarán answered, trying to calm the king.

On the field, Aindrias charged down the barrier towards his opponent, their lances shattering as each made contact with their gritted grand guards.

"Another point rewarded to each competitor," the herald announced.

While they waited for the knights to ready themselves for the third pass, the steward turned back to the warlock.

"Tell us, is this your first individual joust tournament? You must excuse me, your name is Orlynd, is it not?" Ciarán inquired.

"Aye."

"I see. Then, perhaps, may I suggest to His Grace that he educate his young advisor?" Ciarán proposed.

"You may certainly not!" Francis glared at Ciarán. "Who do you think I am? I am the King, not some nursemaid meant to educate waifs. I will excuse your outburst since my son will be marrying your daughter."

"Yes, Your Grace. I apologise."

Francis smiled slightly, then quickly turned away.

At the same time, Aindrias charged down the barrier towards his opponent. This time Antonio's lance shattered while Aindrias's lance missed.

"Two points for Antonio," the herald announced.

Francis turned his attention to Ciarán.

Feeling Francis's eyes on him, Ciarán took in a deep breath, and said, "Prepare to be amazed, young warlock! Jousting has been the tradition of this country for centuries during times of peace. It was once used for military training, but now has evolved as a sport competition, allowing nobles to demonstrate who is the mightiest and the bravest. There are some basic rules. First, the competitor must be a noble from Vandolay or Glendalow; commoners are only permitted to be spectators."

"Whit about warlocks from Aracelly?" Orlynd asked.

"Your Majesty?" Ciarán asked, looking for assistance in the explanation.

Francis rolled his eyes. "They were once permitted to joust, until too many were caught manipulating the game using their magic."

"Ah see," said Orlynd.

"Second, each noble must provide his own equipment and horse. The squire is the only person permitted to provide a new lance if it should break, speak between charges, and help the competitor up if he should become unhorsed. Third, if the noble is successful in de-horsing his opponent, the match is declared over, and the victor may claim his opponent's armour and horse."

"He may also hold his opponent at ransom if he should so wish," Francis interjected, grinning.

Ciarán nodded in acknowledgement and continued. "Points are awarded as follows: If a lance breaks at the chest and between saddle and helm, one point is given. If a lance breaks at the helm or base, it is two points, and if a competitor should become unhorsed or drop their lance, it is three points. Do you understand?"

"Aye."

"Now, please observe the knight's attire," Ciarán said. "Their armour is constructed from the finest mail, accompanied by a solid, heavy helmet, called a great helm, and mighty shields composed to take the hardest blows."

With a wink Francis teased, "There's even a little extra padding at the rear for when they get de-horsed. I do hope you have a stomach strong enough to handle violence. These things do tend to occasionally get gory."

At that moment, the crowd's cheering increased, and the king's guard readied his lance and charged his opponent, knocking Antonio quickly off his horse and onto the ground.

Francis applauded. "Splendid! Another victory for Aindrias. He makes the other knights on the list look like fools."

Orlynd gazed at the fallen knight with concern, hearing him moan on the ground in pain. "Yir Grace, is that man injured?"

"Never mind, the squire will attend to him."

Unable to accept this embarrassment, the knight stood back on his feet, revealed a small knife from underneath his armour and threw it towards his opponent, hitting the horse. The horse neighed and stood on its back legs, knocking Aindrias onto the ground.

"Seize that man!" Francis commanded. "How dare his frustration be taken out on an innocent horse!"

"I will see the knight is rightfully punished, Your Grace," Ciarán stated. He stood up from his chair and walked over to where guards had surrounded Antonio. "Take him away!"

The remainder of the afternoon went without incident. By the time it had come for the prince's appearance, the field had been narrowed down to one remaining knight, Aindrias, who, other than having a sore back from being thrown from his horse a few times, was eager for the prince's challenge. He had obtained better armour and a faster horse.

Déor appeared from his tent to the eruption of the spectators' applause, riding on Arthelea, a magnificent white horse with brown patches that was already attuned to the competition. The prince smiled and lifted his right hand to greet everyone.

"Aindrias," Déor mused while the squire approached with a lance. "I cannot think of a worthier opponent. My father chose well in the selection of his guard."

"Thank you, Your Grace," Aindrias replied. "I am honoured to accept your challenge."

Déor grinned and lifted his lance into the air, to the crowd's applause. He trotted over to the Royal Box.

"My lady, would you kindly do me the honour?" Déor requested, reaching his lance out towards Anya so she could tie a ribbon from her hair to symbolise that Déor represented her in the competition.

"My prince," Anya answered with a slightly higher pitch, keeping her eyes fixed on his.

"Please, accompany me to the viewing stand for the Lady of the Joust."

CHAPTER EIGHT

MCKINNON ESTATE
GLENDALOW
1238 CE

Mierta approached the oversized bogwood door with a cast iron latch, which led to the cellar. He could feel his heart rapidly beating in his chest in anticipation. What would he find down there? Would he be able to locate the elixir book? More importantly, would he even be able to understand any of it? The book had to be salvageable, otherwise Lord Kaeto wouldn't have even mentioned it. He was meant to have this book; he just had to find it.

He reached into his breeches pocket and pulled out the old-fashioned key his father had given him the day before. Turning it over, he noticed its rustic features; it felt cold and heavy in his hand.

"All right. Show me your secrets," Mierta spoke to the key, grinning.

He reached up and placed the key into the keyhole. He tried to turn the lock, but it wouldn't budge. Years of disuse had somehow caused the lock to become frozen. Unwilling to give up, he tried again, turning it counterclockwise until he heard the bolt slide away. With anticipation growing, he quickly unfastened the latch and pulled it toward him. The door opened with a loud creak. A musty, mildewed aroma filled his nostrils, and an intense, cool draft emerged from below, sending a chill down his spine.

Mierta stared into absolute darkness, listening for any kind of sound or movement. Cautiously, he reached into his pocket and pulled out his wand.

"Scamos lias," Mierta commanded.

A dim, turquoise, florescent light sparkled from the tip of his wand. With a slight ache in his heart, Mierta silently thanked his mum for teaching him simple spells.

Mother, I wish you were here. Then we could still be together. I promise you, Mother, I will not stop until I find who killed you, and when I do, he or she will be sorry.

Lifting the wand in front of him carefully, he could see the large cobblestone texture covering the walls and stairs.

"Hello," Mierta spoke softly with a smile, his eyes brightening, not expecting an answer. He lifted his eyebrows and puckered his lips, wondering what secrets he would find below. Cautiously, he placed his foot on the first stair and heard it echo. He paused.

So much for a surprise entrance, Mierta thought to himself.

He took a second step and then a third. However, when he placed his right foot down again, he heard a loud screech from underneath him.

"Ah!" Mierta screamed, flailing his arms while attempting to lift his foot. His wand was sent flying out of his hand as his body twisted and sailed down the remaining stairs until he hit the cherrywood floor with his back, knocking the air out of his lungs and sending huge dust plumes into the air.

"*Oof!*"

Gasping, Mierta looked around, trying to locate his wand. It was shining dimly just a short distance away. He reached out for it, only to discover it was much farther away than he thought.

He stared at his wand intently. Again, overcome by an unknown sensation, the pupils of his eyes took on the shape of snake eyes.

"Convosuri!"

The wand lifted off the ground and flew directly into his hand. Once his hand had firmly grasped his wand, Mierta rolled over onto his stomach and lifted it to illuminate the stairway, his eyes now back to their normal appearance.

"Blimey, what a fall," he said aloud to himself, observing the staircase.

Crinkling his brow and parting his mouth ever so slightly, he spotted what he had stepped on. A rat stared back at him from the stairwell. Mierta returned the stare, uncertain what to do.

The rat then screeched loudly in indignation and disappeared into a hole in the wall.

Mierta lowered his wand and gathered his thoughts. "Rats. Right," he said between breaths, acknowledging his father's warning.

He carefully stood up and brushed the dust off his robe. Repositioning his wand, he shined its light around himself, checking for any tears in the fabric or scrapes on his body. Other than the dust from the floor, he found nothing amiss.

"I need more light," he concluded. "What were the words Mum taught me? *Scamos...scamos...err.*" Mierta tapped the sides of his face while pacing back and forth several times. Abruptly stopping, he turned, raised his wand and shouted, *"Scamos lias luz intensate!"* A huge grin spread on his face when the wand shined a powerful turquoise light, brightening the entire cellar. Proud of himself, he whispered, "Thanks, Mum."

Mierta took in the scene before him. It was nothing like the cellar he had seen in his future. Through a myriad of cobwebs, he could make out three large wooden workbenches. He could just make out shapes on one of the tables, but was unable to see what they were, due to the thick coating of dust that seemed to cover everything. Every step he took produced echoes throughout the cellar and left clouds of dust in his wake.

As he started toward the tables, he stumbled over the body of a long-dead animal.

"Ah!" Mierta cried, his eyes wide, catching himself. Looking down, he observed what he had tripped over.

"Eww!" he reacted, crunching his brow and crinkling his nose, realising it probably had been just another rat. However, its carcass, which was covered in hundreds of dead maggots, had been long since reduced to bones with very little skin remaining.

"Sorry, if the rat on the staircase was your mate," Mierta jested.

Mierta stepped over the carcass, adjusted the front of his robe, and raised his wand, continuing to explore the cellar.

The floor and walls were constructed of river rock and mortar, which were covered in some places by damp moss and mildew, and cobwebs hung prolifically from the ceiling. Lining the walls were several shelves, some of which held books, while others held hundreds of glass bottles, some empty, meant for storage, and some containing ingredients long expired.

Mierta lifted his eyebrows, widened his eyes, and muttered to himself. "Reckon I won't be needing any bottles anytime soon."

He surveyed the rest of the cellar wondering what had made his father abandon his studies. His thoughts became distracted by the workbench he was now standing in front of. A broken jar containing unknown ingredients was scattered over the table and mixed with several inches of dust. "Curious," he thought as he traced his finger through the dust. He tilted his head when he thought he saw what looked like a roll of parchment underneath the chemicals.

"What have we got here?" he asked, his eyes brightening.

Mierta took in a deep breath, leaned forward and blew on the workbench, sending thousands of dust particles into the air, which caused him to cough uncontrollably.

"Must...remind myself...never to do that again," he uttered between coughs. *"Achoo!"* His abrupt sneeze caused more dust to infiltrate the air.

Irritated with himself, Mierta reached for the roll of parchment, only to have it disintegrate in his hand. He quickly dropped the dust from the parchment. Mierta blinked, set his wand down on the workbench, nervously readjusted his robe, and brushed his hands through . his hair.

"How unfortunate, I would have liked to have read that," Mierta said to the workbench. He turned his attention to the bookshelves. "Right. Enough time wasted. Time to find the elixir book." He glanced around the room again, contemplating where to go next.

Then, on another workbench, Mierta spotted a large caldron and two candlestick holders, which stood empty. He scrambled around the cellar, discovering a box of candles. Retrieving two of them, he placed them in the candlesticks.

He picked up his wand from the workbench and pointed it at the candlesticks. *"Sine!"* Mierta exclaimed, setting the candlesticks ablaze. Satisfied, he put his wand back down on the workbench and danced over to the bookshelves to search for the book.

"No," Mierta said after examining a book and throwing it behind him. He grabbed the next book off the shelf, opened it, and after seeing the pictures depicting unclothed bodies, he slammed the book shut.

"No!" he said a bit louder, throwing the book behind him, unable to withhold his disgust.

He reached up again, his hand coming across something brittle. Grasping it, he pulled out a bone, which may have once belonged to a human child. Mierta crinkled his brow, widened his eyes and parted his mouth as he gazed over it. Unable to come up with anything witty, he dropped it beside him.

Next, he came across a book on how to perform minor surgeries. "This might be useful," he said, carefully placing it on the workbench.

Mierta turned back to the bookshelf and pulled the next book off the shelf. Looking it over he recognised his father's handwriting. "Ha! Yes! This is it!" He grinned.

Quickly racing over to the middle workbench, he slammed it on the table. Opening it to the inside cover, he stopped at a message written in ink by his father.

"I hereby pass my first compound book on to my next of kin. May he forever uphold our family's honour after what I've seen in my Rite of Wands."

"The Rite of Wands? What has Father been keeping secret all these years?" Mierta furrowed his forehead, wondering if what he was interpreting as his father's writing was correct. He decided to investigate further, quickly opening the book and glancing at the first recipe. His eyes grew wide. "What? This cannot be," he stammered. "I can't read it."

CHAPTER NINE

COINNEACH CASTLE
THE KINGDOM OF VANDOLAY
1238 CE

Déor stared his opponent down. Because Aindrias was a member of his father's guard, the prince was certain he wouldn't put up much of a challenge, leading to an easy victory.

After all, he was the crown prince, and Aindrias would not dare win the challenge. He exchanged smiles of approval with his father before Arthelea danced and pranced toward the beginning of the track.

Satisfied, Déor lowered his helmet and charged down the barrier towards his opponent. However, when their lances made contact with the gritted guard, a piece of armour attached at the shoulder, Déor's lance was abruptly knocked out of his hand.

The crowd went silent before the herald announced, "Three points for Aindrias."

Once Déor had reached the end of the track, he quickly turned around and raised his helmet, his mouth partially open and eyes wide.

How dare Aindrias embarrass me in front of my people! Déor thought. He could not fathom looking towards the Royal Box, certain his father would be displeased.

"Squire!" Déor shouted, slamming his helmet down and impatiently holding his hand out for his lance. He could not allow further misfortune to spoil this day of celebration.

He raised his lance, took his position at the beginning of the track, and charged. Aindrias missed his mark while Déor's lance shattered at the helm.

"Two points for His Grace."

The prince was now only one point behind. This still did not satisfy him. There was only one thing left for him to do; unhorse his opponent and put an end to this match.

Again, he readied Arthelea at the beginning of the track, took the lance from the squire, and charged.

The crowd gasped. The moment their lances made contact, Déor could feel himself slipping off the left side of the horse. He realised he couldn't grab the reins for the horse might rear up, possibly falling on top of him, resulting in his death. Thinking quickly, and using the stirrups, he recovered, thus preventing further embarrassment.

Francis stood from his chair, seeing both opponents beginning to fall off their horses. He held his breath, watching Déor begin to right himself, letting it out when he noticed Aindrias fall from his.

The spectators' gasps were replaced by a loud applause. Déor gazed around, realising he had been successful in unhorsing Aindrias.

"His Grace wins!"

The tournament concluded with an award ceremony.

When it was the prince's turn, Francis stepped forward and called to his servant to bring forth the box, revealing a small amulet on a chain.

"Congratulations, my son," Francis said. "I hereby reward you with this gift, a family heirloom given to me on my fourteenth birthday by my father, as was given to him on his. May the Bynoch guide and protect you."

It was a clear quartz manifestation crystal, containing a smaller crystal growing within a large one, wrapped in a golden wire, and hung from a silver chain. Stories passed down alleged the Bynoch contained a hidden magic. Created by an old warlock from the Kingdom of Aracelly, it would preserve the lineage of the royal family.

"Thank you, Your Majesty," Déor answered, kneeling as his father placed the gem around his neck.

The king gazed down, expecting the mystery that had eluded him most of his life would be answered. However, the charm appeared to act no differently for his son than it had for him.

"This cannot be," Francis muttered to himself. "The necklace must intercede. He is the last of my line, my only heir. How can my son not be destined to be its master?"

Francis began staring uncomfortably at his son.

"May I rise, Your Majesty?" Déor asked under his breath, startling his father from his thoughts when the king continued to look fixedly at him.

Bewildered, Francis answered, "Yes, of course. Everyone, your prince," he said with a smile.

After Déor had retreated to his tent and Lady Anya had exited the viewing stand, the applause ceased.

Francis continued, "Good people of the realm, and those visiting, I hope you found today's tournament entertaining and enjoyable. Our celebration continues in the Great Hall for food, drinks and merriment."

"Yir Grace!" Orlynd urged, following the king down the stairs, distracting him from his troubled thoughts. He lowered his voice to avoid commotion, watching the spectators make their way past them in the direction of the Great Hall. "Ah beg ay yis for a private audience."

"Now is not the time," Francis said.

"Yir Grace, yis dinnae understand," Orlynd uttered anxiously. "Ah must insist. Yir son must nae marry Lady Anya," Orlynd said, his voice breaking.

"And may I inquire why?" Francis asked, turning back, quickly losing his patience. "Are you indicating you know something I do not?"

"Aye, Ah believe so, Yir Grace," Orlynd answered urgently. "Ah huv reason tae believe yir lives ur in grave danger."

Francis's eyes grew wide. "What evidence do you have of this? Have there been rumours of this ill deed spreading through my court? I demand an explanation. Speak!" he said.

Orlynd cringed when the king shouted at him. Sweat was beginning to trickle down his back. "Forgive me Yir Grace, but hear me out," he stated nervously. "When the Lady Anya first made her appearance, Ah foresaw someone pouring poison into the royal goblet."

"And?"

Orlynd could feel his heart thumping in his temples. "N Ah believe yis will drink it," he spoke between gasps.

Francis moved in closer to the warlock, stating sternly yet quiet enough to avoid a commotion, "Do you dare to accuse Lady Anya of such a crime?"

"Nae, Yir Grace," Orlynd stated quickly, frightened by the king's attitude. "Ah…"

Francis breathed in a slow breath in order to calm himself; however, his looks betrayed him. "Heed my warning. In this kingdom, false accusation of murder against the crown is an act of treason. You may have been able to convince me you had the gift of foresight, but I'd be careful of what you are uttering. It is one thing to predict events, but it is another to accuse someone of noble blood of treason! Take care, warlock, or it may be your head that meets the guillotine next." The king turned his back to the soothsayer. "Now, I am going to enjoy the rest of the evening without further outbursts. Do not make me question your loyalty again!"

Frozen, Orlynd stood watching the king continue onward. Spectators nearby made their way around the warlock, some even shoving him out of the way.

"Aye, Yir Majesty," he mumbled, crestfallen.

MCKINNON ESTATE
GLENDALOW
1238 CE

"MONSIEUR?" ARMAND said, after entering the main hall. He was surprised to find the cellar door open and Mierta stopped at the top of the staircase. "Forgive me, I did not expect to find you up and about. Your father said you were ill and should be resting."

Mierta, cradling the elixir book in his right arm, stared at his father's servant with a bit of annoyance. "I thank you for your concern, Armand, but I am fine," he answered, matter-of-factly.

"I am glad to hear that, good Monsieur. I just finished setting the kettle on the stove to brew some of your favourite tea. Shall I bring a cup to your room when it is ready?"

"Yes, thank you," Mierta answered with a small smile, wishing Armand would stop talking so he could begin unravelling the mystery behind whatever concealed the vital information required to access the book. He waited until Armand allowed him to pass.

"Have I said something wrong, Monsieur? You look upset," Armand said.

"How long have you known my father, Armand?" he asked.

Armand, taken aback by the question, looked up toward the ceiling as he recalled. "My parents sold me to your family five years ago."

Mierta nodded. "And have you ever seen him go into this cellar?" He questioned, pointing in the direction of the cellar.

"No, Monsieur," Armand responded.

"What about this?" Mierta demanded a bit urgently, revealing the book from under his arm, holding it out in front of him and shaking it at his servant. "Have you seen this book before?"

Armand glanced down at the book and its title. "No, Monsieur. Is there a problem?"

"Problem?!" Mierta bellowed. "The problem is I can't read it! Lord Kaeto told me I needed to find this book and I did, but it's no use," he said. If he couldn't figure this out how was he supposed to prevent what he saw in his Rite of Wands? He needed to get started now! Mierta's heart sank; he would have to wait for his father to return and hope he would be able to help.

"I am afraid I do not understand, Monsieur. Is it in a different language? If it is in French, I can interpret it for you."

"Thank you, Armand, but you can't help me. Not unless you know how to break a charm," Mierta answered, miserably.

"A charm, Monsieur?"

"Yes, a charm, a spell, reckon it makes the contents of this book illegible to whoever attempts to read it. It's as if something is trying to prevent me from finding out what I need to know, only I don't know how to reverse it," Mierta said, beside himself.

"I'm sorry, Monsieur, I do not know anything about magic, but I believe the spell book your father keeps in his bedroom might be of assistance."

"What?" Mierta stated with a look of confusion.

"I've seen it myself, Monsieur," Armand confirmed. "He keeps it underneath his bed."

Why would my father have need for a book of spells, let alone store it in his room? He can't cast them. It would be of no use to him.

Mierta concluded the spell book must have once belonged to his mother, and his father had probably decided to hide it until he felt his son was ready for it, just like he had with the cellar key. A grin filled Mierta's face.

He spun around, snapped his fingers and pointed at his father's servant. "Armand, you are brilliant! If I haven't said it enough, you are absolutely brilliant! You must show me the location of this spell book right away!"

"Oui, Monsieur, as soon as I have finished brewing your tea."

CHAPTER TEN

COINNEACH CASTLE
THE KINGDOM OF VANDOLAY
1238 CE

Night had fallen, and the elaborate Great Hall of Coinneach Castle had filled with guests eager for a feast fit for a king, along with the music and dancing of a magnificent ball.

The massive banquet hall floor was made of Carrera marble. A portion of the floor had been set aside for those wishing to dance to the violinist's wonderful music. Various swords and shields representing knights and warriors from Iverna's history were strategically displayed on the walls. Adjacent to each side of the room were two large tables filled from end to end with delicious food selections, including civet of hare, stag, stuffed chicken and a loin of veal. Pheasants adorned with their feathers were positioned in the middle of each table. At the head of the hall was a separate table designated for the king, the prince, Lady Anya, and the Lord High Steward.

"Mortain!" Francis exclaimed after Déor and Anya had joined the dancing, and the Lord High Steward had engaged in conversation with the prime minister. His court physician's attempt to avoid being seen while entering the Grand Hall had miserably failed.

"Your Grace," Mortain smiled, turning around. He made his way to the table and bowed.

"I am delighted you arrived in time for the festivities," Francis said, midway through his meal, smiling, after having helped himself to another sip of ale.

"Thank you, Your Grace. I am happy to be in your presence. Please accept my apologies for missing the jousting event. I heard the prince did well."

"I feared you would be delayed by your son's Rite of Wands ceremony. I presume he has been awarded his magical gift?" Francis asked, reaching for a slice of stag.

"Yes." Mortain smiled. "It was not easy; however, I am confident Mierta will succeed as a warlock. Reckon in a few years, I will be anxiety-ridden all over again when Lochlann is old enough to participate," he said, between laughs.

Francis nodded, satisfied. "I am certain you are capable of raising the boys correctly, so that may be. Please, accept my condolences for the recent loss of your wife."

"Thank you," Mortain replied, his expression turning to sadness.

"I am confident justice will be served and the criminals responsible will be found."

Mortain nodded, although he did not share the same confidence. He decided to change the subject and cleared his throat. "Your Grace, I have heard discussion through members of your court you have taken on a new advisor?"

"Aye," Francis sighed, taking a bite of hard bread. "Celeste O'Brien's boy, though to be honest, I am beginning to question his loyalty."

"I see. May I inquire where the young warlock might be now?"

"How in Hades should I know? I am not his wet nurse!" Francis barked. "I understand you were good friends with the warlock's father. Tell me, in your experience, is the boy trustworthy?"

"Yes, I would believe so," Mortain replied. "Though I confess I have had very little association with his son."

"Pity," Francis said, finishing off a large handful of grapes and throwing the empty stem aside. "I was hopeful you would be able to provide your opinion of the young warlock. Especially after you welcomed the opportunity to…"

"I'm confident Your Highness will determine the boy's honesty," Mortain interrupted, his pulse increasing.

Francis furrowed his brows. "Perhaps. It matters not. I gather there is something else you wish to discuss."

"Why, yes, Your Grace," Mortain said, heat rising to his cheeks. "I request approval, so when the time comes and I am no longer capable of being in your service, my son, Mierta, may become successor as court physician."

Francis looked up with concern, studying Mortain's face. "Have you taken ill? Why wasn't I informed?"

Mortain shook off the king's sentiment. "You needn't be worried, Your Grace. My health is fine. Mierta has proven he shares my love of medicines, and I am eager to teach him everything I know."

"I am pleased of this news. However, I must evaluate his ability before granting your request. I do not wish to have someone who is incompetent or has no interest."

"I understand," Mortain responded.

Francis eyed him. "I have decided when your boy is ready to begin his apprenticeship, you may bring him to my court."

"Thank you, Your Grace. You are most kind. Reckon that shall be sooner than later. Mierta has already started exploring simple recipes of ingredients to compound."

"Is that so? Correct me if I am mistaken, Mortain, but your son is only twelve years of age, is he not?"

"Why, yes, Your Grace."

"Is it your belief that Mierta desires an apprenticeship now?"

"Yes, that I do believe."

"And would it be necessary to appoint an apprenticeship for Mierta? I believe Ezekiel Kavanagh, our local Apothecarist, has recently returned from teaching in Edesia. He should be satisfactory," Francis said.

"I am honoured by Your Majesty's generous offer, but it shall not be necessary. Mierta will be more than happy to learn from his father."

"Very well, then, it shall be. I invite your son to Vandolay as soon as it can be arranged. He shall be under your fine tutelage. I expect to see great things from him."

"Thank you, Your Grace."

"The thanks are mine," Francis answered, standing, suddenly feeling ill, wondering if he had consumed too much ale. "I regret having to take my leave of the festivities. I have enjoyed myself, perhaps a bit too much." The king grabbed his goblet, "I must admit I am not getting any younger. I shall retire to my chambers to rest. I bid everyone a goodnight."

CHAPTER ELEVEN

MCKINNON ESTATE
GLENDALOW
1238 CE

All right, show me where it is!" Mierta spoke to Armand, his eyes twinkling.

Armand pointed into Mortain's bedroom. "It's in there, Monsieur—underneath the bed."

Uncertain, Mierta slowly sidestepped into the bedroom, his lips slightly open, as if he were expecting his father to show up at any moment to scold him. The room was twice the size of his own.

Why shouldn't it be? He questioned himself. *It is the master bedroom after all.*

Looking around the room, Mierta saw two small tables covered in papers and books. One had a candlestick on it containing a half-burned candle in it. The other had a stack of papers with a quill and inkpot which had been knocked on its side.

"That's rather unfortunate," Mierta said to the room. "Ink can be scarce."

There didn't seem to be any organisation to the books or the papers as if it was purposely stacked that way to keep out snoopers.

"I can't be bothered with that now. I have a more important book to find."

He approached the side of the bed, got down on his hands and knees and peeked into the space underneath the bed. Seeing nothing unusual, he stated, "Armand, there's nothing there. Are you sure?"

"Oui, Monsieur. I'm certain it is under there," Armand assured. "I've seen him placing something under there. Do you think there may be an invisibility spell on it?"

"That's rubbish. My father is a court physician, not a warlock. He would have no interest with enchantments," Mierta countered, beginning to get agitated. Staring at the edge of the bed, contemplating Armand's suggestion, he decided he would have to crawl underneath and investigate further. He removed his wand from the pocket of his breeches, got on his hands and knees and turned towards Armand. "I'm going to have a look. Stay there."

He looked under the bed again and said, *"Scamos lias."* His wand lit up and he crawled underneath. Quickly adjusting his body into a kneeling position, he promptly hit himself on the head. "Ouch!"

"You all right, Monsieur?"

"I'm fine," Mierta answered. "Bed's lower than it appears."

I'm such a klutz, Mierta thought to himself.

"Be careful, Monsieur," cautioned Armand.

Mierta lowered himself just enough as to not knock his head again and started looking around. He noticed a board, which appeared to be just slightly higher than the others around it. Running his hand over it he realised it was indeed out of place. "Armand, you clever fellow! There's a board here that's positioned just slightly at an angle. I reckon the spell book is located right underneath it!"

Mierta tried to grasp the board with his hands; however, there was just enough of the board for him to get his fingernails on. He pulled gently at first, unsuccessfully. Repositioning himself, he pulled a little harder. The board stubbornly refused to give.

"Blimey!" he exclaimed, starting to feel sweat form on his brow. "It hadn't occurred to me that it would be this difficult."

"What's that, Monsieur?" Armand asked, only catching pieces of what Mierta had said.

Mierta poked his head out from underneath the bed. "I cannot get a proper grip on the board. I reckon it's stuck," he said, ducking back under.

"Do you need assistance with it, Monsieur? I can probably loosen it for you."

"No, no, I got it," Mierta answered, moving directly over the board. He braced his back against the underside of the bed, and using both hands, pulled one final time. "Argh!" he exclaimed, finally getting the floorboard to loosen its grip. Embarrassed, he looked in both directions with just his eyes, before he lifted the board with ease.

"You all right, Monsieur?"

"Yes, I'm fine. I'm fine," Mierta answered, placing the board down beside him. He then stared down into the darkness. An aroma of grass, acid, and a hint of vanilla over an underlying mustiness filled his nostrils.

Holding his wand over the open area, he glanced down. An ancient looking spell book lay at the bottom of the space. He reached down with his free hand and lifted the book from its grave, blowing the tiny particles of dust into the air. The cover was made of leather which had been dyed blue. The binding was hand stitched and the book was held closed by a small silver latch. The cover contained a variety of designs. There didn't seem to be any rhyme or reason to the swirls and squiggles on the front cover; however, there was a beauty to it nonetheless.

On the back, he saw two identical dragons facing each other.

Lord Kaeto! I wonder what happened to the rest of his kin.

Mierta imagined the book had once been magnificent, but what remained was a shell of what it used to be—cracked, threadbare, and peeling with age. The pages within were quite yellow; Mierta was almost afraid to open the delicate looking tome.

As he held his wand over the spell book in his hand, he felt what only could be described as a sudden sense of comfort.

"Mum?" he uttered, staring at the cover, furrowing his forehead.

Why was this buried under here? Is there some secret in here no one should know?

There was no doubt in his mind, this had to be the book he had been searching for. However, further investigation of the book's contents was needed, and under the bed was not the place. He replaced the board.

With determination in his eyes, Mierta shook the light out of his wand, placing it back into the pocket of his breeches, and gathered the book under his arm.

This book, whatever the reason, would no longer be permitted to be hidden from him. He would hide it too if he had to, though he wasn't sure exactly how he would do so.

Perhaps there is an invisibility charm in this book I can master.

However, he shortly realised a new problem would arise—even if he could cast such a spell on the book, it would become hidden from him too. Instead, he decided to trust his inner feelings.

He slid from underneath the bed, stood up, and brushed the dust from his breeches. He stared at his family's servant as he approached him. "Thank you, Armand, for your assistance. I trust you won't inform my father I have found this book."

"Oui, of course, young Monsieur," Armand replied.

"I'm going to take it to my room now. I need to rest," Mierta said.

Once he had reached his room, he closed the door behind him and hurried to his bed.

Grinning, he plopped the book down and opened it. His grin was soon replaced with a frown of surprise and disappointment at what he discovered. The opening page, had been ripped out, leaving behind a rough edge.

Mother, what happened? Why was this page removed?

He turned to the next page.

Words were written in quill ink next to an illustration of a dresser drawer being opened: *Obrate combriando.*

"O bra te com bree on doe?" Mierta sounded out the words, scratching his head. "I reckon I should give it a go," he spoke out loud. He brought his wand back out and pointed it towards a dresser positioned across from his bed. *"Ohbratay combriando,"* he said. When the wand did not respond, he tried again with more confidence, *"Obrate combriando!"*

As depicted, the drawers to his dresser opened.

He laughed, pleased with the result. He looked down at the word again for confirmation and glanced back up at his accomplishment. "Oh, that's brilliant! What other devious spells are in here?"

He flipped the page and continued flipping it until he came upon a spell with a warning next to it.

"What's this?" he said, licking his lips. "Do not attempt. What kind of bollocks is this?"

He strained his vision trying to read the very small words. *"Ki boo nika lock due flam bay?* Wait, what? Someone was not right bothered, what a waste."* He shrugged his shoulders, picked up his wand and pointed it towards the wall.

"Kibunika lac du flambé." A small spark sizzled from the end of his wand but seemed to go out before it even began. Perplexed, Mierta raised his wand and chanted again, *"Kibunika lac du flambé!"*

Another small spark shot from his wand, then went out. "What's wrong with you?" Mierta asked his wand while rubbing a hand through his hair, causing it to stand up straight. "I hope I haven't broken it," he said aloud. "Perhaps I am pronouncing the words wrong."

Abruptly his hand twitched, feeling a surge of power coming from the wand that he couldn't explain. Gripping it with both of his hands, he watched amazed as a ball of turquoise energy shot out from the tip.

"Obrate combriando!" yelled Mierta, his bedroom door obeying his command by opening.

Next, the ball of energy bounced off the adjacent wall and flew out of his room.

"No! No! No!" Mierta shouted, eyes wide. "I'm so daft! Why didn't I consider that happening?" His eyes grew wider as he heard what sounded like it bouncing off the walls in the hallway. "Father's statue! Oh, please, don't."

His words were cut short when he heard the sound of something shattering. He grimaced. "Right. I should have expected that, too."

He was adjusting the front of his robe when the sound of Lochlann crying from his crib made him stop abruptly. "Lochlann's room is still open! I've got to find a way to stop this thing! I can't allow it to hurt my baby brother!"

He jumped out of bed and raced into the hallway.

"Hang on, Lochlann! Don't be scared! Your big brother is on his way!" He managed to close Lochlann's bedroom door just before the energy arrived. It bounced off the door and shot further down the hallway.

Mierta gasped.

"The door to the cellar! I forgot to close it!"

Meanwhile, Armand was approaching from the staircase below with a cup of tea, hearing the commotion coming from upstairs.

"Armand, get down!" Mierta warned.

"Young Monsieur?" Armand questioned, ducking down, feeling his hair blow from what felt like a sudden wind.

"Out of the way!" Mierta said, accidentally brushing against Armand, and causing the cup of tea in his hand to spill all over the step. "Sorry!" Mierta called, in his hopeful attempt at catching the energy as it shot towards the floor below them. "I'm so sorry! No time to explain, very urgent I stop this!"

He raced to the cellar door, slamming it shut after the energy went inside. Soon afterward he could hear the sound of multiple jars breaking.

"*Ooo! Ah! Eee!*" Mierta winced at each shattering he heard. "That's going to take a while to clean up. I hope there's a spell in the book to reverse all of this and help me fix the statue upstairs. I don't know how I will explain everything to Father otherwise." He raced back up the stairs to his room, grabbed the book and frantically looked for a spell that would stop the energy ball.

CHAPTER TWELVE

COINNEACH CASTLE
THE KINGDOM OF VANDOLAY
1238 CE

O rlynd entered Tower Chainnigh, following what seemed like an endlessly winding stone staircase. The stairs were attached to the walls of the tower with the centre open to the air. Looking down into the centre was like looking into a dark abyss. Orlynd tried not to look for too long, as it made him feel dizzy. He could not imagine what would happen if he fell into it. A faint light appeared in an open doorway just before he reached the bottom.

Passing through the doorway, Orlynd felt like he had entered a different world. Stepping further into the book-filled room, he was awed by the wonder he saw. The cavernous room had bookshelves as far as the eye could see. There were tables and chairs stationed between the bookshelves, some of which were covered in papers and scrolls. In the very centre of the room was a sculpture of the known universe made from an unfamiliar metal.

"May I help you with something?" a woman asked, startling the warlock. "I do beg your pardon, but you seem to be distracted."

Startled, Orlynd looked over and saw an older woman standing very near him. She wore a heavily embroidered dress in dark brown tones with light blue accents. He could not determine her hair colour as her head was covered in a cloth crown matching the dress, with a light brown veil flowing down over her shoulders.

"Nae, Ah dinnae know. At least Ah dinnae believe so," Orlynd said, nervously.

"I understand. Wanderers often find their way up here. This is one of three towers found at Coinneach Castle. It is a good place to come when one is trying to let go of one's troubles."

"Aye," Orlynd nodded. "It is quiet n Ah can interpret ma thoughts."

The woman smiled. "I'm glad you approve. May I inquire what brought you down here? Perhaps you were looking for a particular scroll?"

"Eh…eh… Ah dinnae know whit Ah am supposed tae dae. Ma family is gone. Ah huv nothing, but eywis clothes oan ma back. His Majesty has been generous, n this kingdom has become ma new hame, but Ah dinnae believe Ah belong here anymore."

"May I suggest you need someone to confide in? Anything you may say will be kept confidential."

"Nae," Orlynd shook his head. "Ah huv said tae much. Besides, Ah already stated whit wis necessary tae whom Ah needed tae n they disregarded me. Sorry. Ah should be leaving."

"Very well," the woman smiled warmly, pointing. "If you change your mind, there are seats and tables available alongside the wall. Take all the time you wish. My name is Beatrice. The library is yours to explore as long as you'd like."

"Yis ur very kind. Ma name is Orlynd."

"Orlynd?" Beatrice said as if the name channelled a memory. "Oh my stars! I thought you looked familiar when you first came in. Please excuse me, I should have recognised your Lorritish burr. My memory tends to sometimes fail me. You are Orlynd O'Brien, are you not?"

"Aye?" Orlynd answered, confused.

"I do not expect you to recognise me. My goodness, it has been a long time. Please accept my condolences on the loss of your mother. Celeste was such a beautiful and kind woman. She was always good to me. Your father on the other hand—a bit chippy, if I recall."

"Ah'm sorry, who ur yis?"

"Oh, I do beg your pardon! I'm getting carried away again," Beatrice said between giggles, her cheeks growing pink. "I should expect you to not recognise me. Why, you were just a wee babe the last time I saw you. My, it is good to see you again! Have a seat at the table in the corner, and I will explain everything to you."

Orlynd did as Beatrice instructed and waited for her to join him.

Several minutes later, Beatrice emerged with a large book in her hand and sat down at the opposite end of the table. "There, I couldn't forget to bring this. It's a registry of everyone who has served in this castle." She flipped through the book. "Ah, yes. See? There's your name right there."

"Ah'm sorry, who ur yis again?" Orlynd questioned.

Beatrice looked over at Orlynd and cleared her throat. "Yes, my name is Beatrice Calderon, and I am the keeper of records in Tower Chainnigh. I have served His Majesty Francis, and the Queen Mother before him. As I'm sure you already know, your mother was King Francis's soothsayer. What you do not know is I helped her to give birth to you in the royal carriage before our arrival in Poveglia. Celeste was in this very tower, searching for a scroll when her contractions began. I recall your father insisting she give birth in Vandolay; however, she would hear none of it. It was important to her that you had the opportunity to receive your magical inheritance. You see, I knew then that someday you were destined to return to this castle! Once we crossed the border into the Kingdom of Aracelly, you could not wait to make your appearance! Tell me, do you have your mother's gift of foresight?"

"Aye," Orlynd answered.

"I'm so pleased to hear that. King Francis has been, how can I word this, beside himself, since Celeste died. I'm certain His Majesty's heart was warmed at your arrival."

"Ah gen up doubt it. Ma father wis exiled n His Majesty only accepted me because ay ma mam. Ah'm nothing but a burden tae him. It wis a mistake. Ma father should never huv brought me tae court."

"I beg to differ. Your father wasn't mistaken in bringing you to court. He was guided by God. You have as much of a right to be here as anyone else, and perhaps more so."

"Ah dinnae understand."

Beatrice gasped, "Oh, you poor lad!" she sympathised. "You have no knowledge of your mother's family history, do you?"

Orlynd stared back at her, bewildered.

"I thought so. Stay right here. There is something you should see," Beatrice said, standing up.

Orlynd watched as she headed towards one of the bookshelves on the opposite side of the room. "Now, where did I file that book?" he could hear her say to the room. "Oh! There it is."

"Yes, now, there you are," Beatrice answered, returning back to the table, opening the book. "Now, where was it? Oh yes, here's the chapter." She flipped to the middle of the large history book until it came upon the page about a previous member of the King's Guard. He was dressed in armour of the time and he was carrying a sword in his hand. "As you can see, Orlynd O'Brien, you are no commoner. I assure you, your father was well aware of your mother's family's infamous descendant. That descendant's blood runs through your veins. You, my dear, are a noble."

Before Orlynd had an opportunity to comprehend what he was looking at, he heard something abrasive and loud coming from above them. "Whit is thit sound?"

Beatrice gasped and placed her hand over her mouth, not wanting to believe what she was hearing.

"Whit is thit?" Orlynd questioned anxiously, speaking louder, believing Beatrice hadn't heard him.

"Lord, have mercy!" Beatrice uttered. Looking up, Orlynd followed her glance. Her cheery expression was replaced by sadness. "Dark times have struck our kingdom," she answered, glancing back over at him. "Those are the bells from the top of this tower. They only ring when someone in the castle has died."

"Whit?"! Orlynd cried. "Nae, it cannae be!" He stood from his chair. "King Francis!"

"Where are you going?"

"Back tae the castle!" shouted Orlynd, running towards the staircase.

MCKINNON ESTATE
GLENDALOW
1238 CE

MIERTA STARED at the cellar door, holding his wand at the ready. He breathed in deeply.

"Okay, Mierta, you can do this," he told himself, letting out a slow breath. "You just need to open the door, go down the stairs, find the energy, err, *Kibunika*, and according to Mum's book, banish it with this spell—*Aboterrar*. Right."

Convincing himself he was prepared, he unfastened the cast iron latch and pulled the door toward him. Once again, he was welcomed by the sound of the creaking door and was instantly reminded of the cellar's musty smell.

"*Scamos lias!*" he commanded his wand. The familiar dim tur-quoise fluorescent glow lit his way down into the darkness.

Careful to not make the same mistake as the previous time and step on any rats, Mierta stared at his feet before proceeding to the next step. When he reached the bottom, all he could hear was silence, not even the sound of a rat scurrying about.

How strange. I wonder if it's possible the Kibunika *could have run out of energy and destroyed itself?*

He turned his head only to see the *Kibunika* coming right for him. "Ah!" he gasped, feeling his heart start to race. He hastily tried to shake his light out of his wand before the *Kibunika* hit him, but he was too late.

"Ugh!" he screamed, feeling himself being knocked backwards after the direct hit to his chest. Once he landed on the floor, the light from his wand promptly went out. His back screamed, and his lungs felt like they did not want to move. He could feel the back of his head pounding, and for a brief moment, his vision blurred as the world spun rapidly around him. It felt like he had been lying there forever, and when he finally sat up, he felt a bit dazed, not recalling what had just happened. However, he was soon reminded when he spotted the *Kibunika* above him.

"Ah!" Mierta exclaimed rolling over before the *Kibunika* struck the floor, leaving a dent in the ground. It bounced back up into the air. Mierta stared at it wide-eyed as it came barrelling down upon him again.

"No! Stop! Ah!" he exclaimed again, rolling over the opposite direction, hearing it crash against the floor and bounce back up into the air and restore itself for another swift blow. He briefly looked down at his wand in his hand, and with resolve, he reached up and pointed it at the *Kibunika*, yelling, "*Aboterrar!*" He watched as the *Kibunika* expeditiously burst into small pieces and dissolved into the air. He slowly lowered his wand to the floor and breathed a sigh of relief.

"Blimey!" Mierta said, breathing heavily as he stood back on his feet. "Next time I read 'do not attempt,' I am going to listen! I could have gotten myself killed."

COINNEACH CASTLE
THE KINGDOM OF VANDOLAY
1238 CE

DREAD FILLED Orlynd's heart as he climbed up the stone stairs.

"Please dinnae let it be the king! Please dinnae let it be the king!" he uttered, reaching the top. He stepped through the access to the courtyard and stopped; going around to the main entrance would take far too long to get to the royal wing. He concluded it would be quicker running across the lush green lawn of the castle's square-shaped courtyard and cut through the kitchen corridor, which connected to the picture gallery where he had first encountered Prince Déor.

Running till he thought his lungs would burst, he reached the Bumbling Staircase. It got its name from the awkward design and shape of the castle's architecture. The staircase contained carvings of naturalistic foliage and small animal detail. He followed another series of twists and turns before reaching the top. Stopping at the top of the staircase to catch his breath, he noticed a female servant coming out of the king's private apartment down the hall, hardly able to contain herself.

"Nae," Orlynd's heart broke. How could it have happened so soon, and why didn't anyone notice anything out of the ordinary?

Preparing himself for what was to come, Orlynd slowly approached the private apartment, noticing the doors were wide open, which Francis would have never permitted. Passing through the room where he had last seen his father, he approached the blue room.

Before him was the king's massive ornately carved wooden bed, and on the floor on the foreside of the bed, lay the king's body.

Prince Déor was already kneeling beside his father's body and weeping.

"Father! Father, please, wake up!" he cried.

Melancholy filled Orlynd's heart. It deeply saddened him that this would be the first time he felt like he could understand the prince's grief.

"Ah'm sorry, Yir Grace," Orlynd said, reaching out to comfort him.

However, Déor would have none of it, and aggressively shoved him away. "Don't touch me, warlock!" he said, turning his face briefly around, tears falling down his face. There was a mix of pain and anger in his voice.

"This is all your fault! You were supposed to be my father's sooth-sayer. You should have known!"

Taken aback, Orlynd found himself on the defence, "Yir Grace, Ah tried," Orlynd started to say, his voice breaking. He thought better of it.

"What use are you to me? You're nothing but a failure! Get out of my sight before I throw you out!" Déor screamed. His attention was drawn to the door as someone else joined them. "Court physician," Déor said, turning towards Mortain. "Please, I beg of you. You can save him. I know you can!"

"Allow me to examine him, Your Grace," Mortain requested, kneeling down besides the king.

He observed a grey-blue tone had already taken to the king's skin, and his eyes were open, stopped and unmoving. Already knowing what to expect, he reached to the king's neck to check for a pulse. There was nothing he could do, he concluded, for the king had been dead for some time and was already beginning to grow cold. As he ventured a little closer to the body, he noted a metallic liquid trickling out of the corners of his mouth.

"Court physician?" the prince begged.

Solemnly, Mortain turned back to Déor. "The King is dead. Long live the King!"

CHAPTER THIRTEEN

MCKINNON ESTATE
GLENDALOW
1238

F ather, you're home!" Mierta exclaimed, throwing himself into his father's arms.

"Blimey, Mierta! You forget I am not getting any younger," Mortain answered, giving Mierta a squeeze. "It is good to be home, though."

"Good afternoon, Mr. McKinnon," Natasha said, appearing from the kitchen. "I thought I recognised your voice."

Natasha was a young woman of average height; her curly dark brown hair was tied up under a white lace kerchief. Her small, round face and short, upturned nose belied her knowledge of rearing babes. Her dress was simple, a flowing white blouse over a flowered skirt, which made it easier for her to go about her duties without being encumbered in any way.

"Good afternoon, Natasha," Mortain replied to Lochlann's wet nurse. "Reckon everything is well?"

"Yes, except for a wee matter concerning little Lochlann," Natasha said. Already preparing for Mortain's next question, she continued. "No need to worry. I'm certain it's because the wee thing has a bit of a cold. However, he's not eating right for me, you see."

Mortain nodded and carefully placed Mierta back onto the floor. "Thank you, Natasha. I will be upstairs momentarily to examine him."

"Tell us, Father, what news of Vandolay?" Mierta asked eagerly. "Was the prince pleased?"

"Yes, well, I'm afraid I bring sombre news," Mortain frowned. "The Hand of the King will be busy arranging a coronation soon I suppose. King Francis is dead—poisoned by someone in his own court, I suspect. I couldn't tell them, though. If I had announced what really happened, it would have sent the entire kingdom into chaos." Mortain quickly decided to change the subject. "Now, enough talk of that. Mierta, did you find the book you were searching for in the cellar? I recall I promised you a lesson in compounding chemicals."

"Yes, it's in my room, but I cannot read it," Mierta responded. "There's some kind of enchantment on it, preventing anyone from being able to read it. I haven't been able to figure it out."

"Is that so?"

"Yes," Mierta answered, staring down at the ground, crinkling his forehead. He felt uncertain whether he should ask his father about the spell.

But, if it is indeed my father's writing in the book, then…

"I don't suppose Mum ever told you where I may be able to find the answer to this spell?"

"Hmm." Mortain thought a moment. "Yes, in fact, I believe the words you are looking for, my boy, are *Arduescha ridícula.*"

"*Are do eshca ree dee coo la?*" Mierta repeated.

So, he really does know spells. But how? I've never seen him with a wand or a magic book or anything of the sort.

"Yes, my boy," Mortain said, interrupting Mierta's thoughts. "Reckon I heard a warlock say it once or twice in Vandolay, passing by."

Mierta stared at his father, doubting his story. He decided against inquiring any further; he would wait till later. His inner instinct told him his father was lying, anyway. Perhaps once he had successfully compounded materials, his father would consider him worthy enough to know the truth.

"Now, I shall be downstairs shortly. Be a good lad and prepare the containers and ingredients you find written on the first page of the elixir book, but do not start without me. Have Armand help you if you get lost. Where has he gone off to this time?" Mortain wondered, shaking his head.

"I had him gather some herbs for you in case you wanted to make a remedy for Lochlann," Natasha said.

"Bless him. Very well, then," Mortain said, turning back to Mierta. "Do you have your wand with you?"

"Yes, Father," Mierta answered, reaching into his breeches to retrieve his wand to show Mortain.

"Good," Mortain replied, smiling. "Well, go on, then. Off you go."

"Cheers!" Mierta grinned at his father before taking off downstairs.

"And don't start without me!" Mortain again called, laughing to himself at Mierta's excitement.

"I don't mean to intrude. But is it true, sir, about the king?" Natasha asked.

"About him being poisoned? Yes, absolutely no doubt about it. I recall he had been complaining of not feeling well before retiring for the night. I suspect the poison by that point was already inside his body creating havoc. There wouldn't have been anything anyone could have done to prevent it, except catch the villain responsible."

"How long do you think it will be before the coronation?"

"Coronation? Ah, well, I reckon the Hand of the King is arranging his daughter's wedding and the coronation as we speak." He turned his attention back to his wet nurse. "That's enough discussion for now. Let us proceed up the stairs and check on Lochlann…"

× ✕ ×

"*SCAMOS LIAS!*" Mierta commanded before hustling down the staircase with the elixir book in one hand and his wand in the other.

After his rather scary encounter with the *Kibunika*, he had been grateful to have the assistance of both Armand and his mother's spell book to successfully reverse the damage done in the cellar and transform it to better conditions. They had righted the workbenches that the *Kibunika* had upended and returned the books to the bookshelves. Armand had grabbed a broom and swept up all the broken jars and dry chemicals on the floor. Mierta had also taken this opportunity to clear out some of the dust and debris that had collected over the years of disuse in the cellar.

Reaching the bottom of the stairs, he sprinted to the middle workbench in the now clean cellar, slamming the elixir book down on it.

"Okay," he said to the room. "Need some better light." He gathered a set of candles and candlesticks along with a cauldron, nearly forgetting there was anyone else in the house.

"Yes, I know!" Mierta said, turning his attention to a rat squeaking and squealing from the staircase. "You don't like how it's all cleaned up. Deal with it! I don't have time for you to have a go at me right now. I have more important engagements."

Shaking the light out of his wand, he pointed it at the first candle. "*Síne!*"

A small fire shot from the wand, lighting the first candle. He repeated this with the remaining candles.

Grinning, he moved to the elixir book. He opened it to the first page, pointed his wand at it, he chanted, "*Arduescha ridícula!*"

He gazed in awe as the letters appeared to travel off the page and dance around in the air before returning to their haven, allowing the words to become comprehendible. "Ha! Brilliant! Shame I hadn't discovered this spell before." He placed the tip of his finger on the page and read the instructions, but quickly became bored.

"There's got to be something better than this in here. There must be something more involved here that I can impress father with," he said, flipping through the book. He read another recipe, flipped the page again before moving on to one that intrigued him.

"Now, what is this? *Acidum salis*—never heard of it, sounds exciting. Reckon I can compound this before father even gets down here! Better get busy, I can't wait to surprise him!"

"THERE, THERE, now, that's better," Mortain comforted Lochlann several minutes later, as the young boy eagerly ate for him. "Reckon he was just missing his dad." He looked up at Natasha and joked, "If only all of my patients were this simple."

"Yes, sir," she agreed.

He turned back to Lochlann. "I'm certain when you're older you won't take any interest in compounding chemicals, will you? Sure wish I knew what your future was going to be."

Mortain startled from what sounded like an explosion coming from the cellar. He suddenly remembered he had offered to teach Mierta how to compound chemicals but had gotten distracted by Lochlann's feeding!

At first, he was annoyed that Mierta had not waited for him, but then his blood ran cold when he heard Mierta's agonising scream.

ARMAND WAS approaching the main house when he felt the ground shake underneath his boots. He abruptly stopped when he heard a muffled explosion.

That's coming from the cellar! Armand thought.

Dropping the herbs, he had collected, Armand took off at a run towards the door. He entered the McKinnon Estate just in time to see his master running down the stairs, towards the cellar door.

CHAPTER FOURTEEN

BRISHEN'S
THE KINGDOM OF ARACELLY
1238

Orlynd stared up at the red sign containing a dragon, which resembled Lord Kaeto, hanging in front of Brishen's, a pub located in the marketplace of the Kingdom of Aracelly. He could hear the sound of laughter coming from inside and the clanking of pints, which helped drown out the obnoxious sound of hammering, nails and wood being constructed in the distance.

It reminded him of the times he was a little boy and would come here with his father. His father had always let him pick out a fresh piece of fruit. He could see those same fruit vendor carts, along with the vegetable carts up the road, had passed onto future generations. However, some other things had remained the same, such as the butcher shop located a bit farther up the road, as well as the shop across the street, where witches and warlocks could get ingredients for their various spells and potions.

Orlynd pushed open the door of the pub and stepped inside. As his eyes adjusted to the dim light, he could see several long tables made of rough wood, mostly filled with patrons, on the left. To the right was a bar made of the same rough wood, stretching the length of the establishment. There were a few patrons standing at the bar drinking and seemingly enjoying themselves.

As he was taking in the scene, he noticed the noise from the patrons had abruptly ceased as they took turns staring at him. His heart dropped. Even in his own kingdom, he could not get away from the stigma of the O'Brien name.

He took a deep breath and approached the bar. Just as he passed, the first patron, an older warlock wearing a long brown tunic, turned and spat at Orlynd's feet. Orlynd ignored the insult and took a seat on a stool at the farthest end of the bar where it was mostly empty.

Orlynd eyed the man behind the bar preparing food and drink for another patron seated at the opposite end of the counter.

"I will be with you shortly," the chubby man said, acknowledging Orlynd. Everyone knew the warlock by the name of Brishen. He had been the owner of the pub for as long as Orlynd could remember. He was wearing a long, dirty white apron over a rough green tunic. His dark brown curly hair and scruffy beard were the same as Orlynd remembered.

"Here is your colcannon, sir," Brishen said, setting down a wooden spoon and bowl in front of the patron. "And your ale." He placed a silver pint mug on the counter and poured ale into it.

Disgusted to be in the presence of Orlynd, the patron picked up his pint and chugged his ale, setting the empty mug down aggressively on the counter before expelling a loud burp.

Brishen ignored the man's rudeness and smiled at Orlynd. "It is very good to see you alive and well, young warlock. News has travelled you have a new role?"

"Aye. Ah'm the King ay Vandolay's new soothsayer, though Ah dinnae think Ah'm very good at it. May Ah inquire whit is all thit noise coming fir outside?"

"Noise?" questioned Brishen, perplexed. "Oh! I'm afraid a wooden gate is being constructed on Dragomir's orders—meant to keep out outsiders, they say."

"Outsiders?" Orlynd gasped. "Since when wis the kingdom ay Aracelly about keeping people out? We ur peacekeepers. We watch over the stone treaty fir the kingdom ay Vandolay!"

"That's true, however, times have changed. Well, ever since that nasty business with the Magulians anyway," Brishen said.

Orlynd cringed at the mention of the Magulians.

"Caught a couple of men from Edesia trying to cause trouble here once. Gave me the impression their king intends on invading our land. Dragomir feels building a gate is the best way to protect our own."

Orlynd tried unsuccessfully to stifle a laugh. "Ah'd like tae see them try. They cannae possibly eliminate us."

"That's what the Magulians thought before your father came along, breaking up their families and sending them out to drown in the sea."

"Ah see." Orlynd's smile turned solemn. "Well," Orlynd cleared his throat. "Ah should take ma leave."

"Already? I'm sorry. I didn't mean any offense. It is at least a three-day journey back to the Kingdom of Vandolay. Certainly, I can offer you lodgings for the night?"

Orlynd stood up from his stool and shook his head. "Ah dinnae know where Ah should be, but it is nae here. Ah wonder if thir will ever come a time when Ah'm nae haunted by whit ma father did."

MCKINNON ESTATE
GLENDALOW
1238 CE

"MIERTA!" MORTAIN shouted at the top of the stairs, hearing nothing but his own voice echo. Watching smoke drifting out of the open doorway, Mortain took in a deep breath and tried to slow down his heart. The aroma of acrid chemicals and burning flesh filled his nose.

"Mierta!" he shouted again. "Son, you all right?" He listened, hearing nothing more than what sounded like gasping breaths.

"Father," Mierta mouthed in response to Mortain's calls, unable to produce any sounds as he dropped to one knee. His heart was pounding. Each pulse matched the ache he felt in his temples. A deep burning pain seared through his chest every time he took a breath. It was like he was slowly being strangled and there was nothing he could do to stop it. The inside of his nose felt charred and his throat felt like he was swallowing tacks. He blinked, his eyesight blurring, the pain beginning to overwhelm him. Nausea built in his throat and droplets of sweat slid down the side of his face. He wished he could do anything to end the torture. He could not imagine dying would be much worse.

Mierta attempted to stand and tried to get away from the workbench. He managed a few staggering steps before his body was drained of all energy. He watched puffy-white circling clouds fill his vision before everything was replaced by darkness.

Mortain felt his stomach drop at the sound of something breaking. "Mierta!" he screamed, racing down the stairs. "Mierta, answer me!"

When he reached the bottom, Mortain abruptly stopped, taking in the horrific scene before him. His son was unconscious, lying sprawled out on his back. What remained of a small culture tube lay shattered next to him, and chemicals dripping from a workbench bubbled and fizzled as they made contact with the hardwood floor.

Acidum salis, he thought, his eyes widening.

Mortain raised his arm to his mouth, careful to not inhale any of the smoke that was filling the room. He trembled as he came closer, observing the damage that had been done to the left side of his son's face.

The skin was mostly raw red with patches of peeling, burned black skin hanging off his face. Blood was seeping from some of the deep crevices caused by the acid. Most of the damage was confined to the cheek and jaw area. His eye was spared any damage.

"Oh, my dear Lord," he uttered, fear filling his heart. "My poor boy! What have I done?"

He placed a finger against the side of Mierta's neck, dreading the worst as he checked for a pulse. He was awarded with a rapid but stable beat.

"Yes, that's good," he whispered to himself, breathing a sigh of relief. "He's still alive. That's very good."

Mortain glanced around spotting where Mierta had last left his wand on the workbench and promptly retrieved it, placing it in his robe before returning.

"Hold on, son," he said, lifting his son's limp body into his arms and carrying him toward the door, a cough escaping him.

I have to get us out of this cloud of chemicals before I also succumb. Mortain thought.

"Armand!" Mortain shouted as he raced up the stairs.

"Oui, Monsieur McKinnon?" Armand said.

"Armand, there's been a terrible accident. I need you to fetch some cloths, a pitcher of cool water, and a basin. Bring them to Mierta's room at once! I fear his life is in grave danger."

"Of course, Monsieur," Armand answered, concern rising in his voice. He watched Mortain rush Mierta up the staircase to his bedroom.

Upon reaching his son's room Mortain laid Mierta on the bed and removed his clothing, leaving on just his undergarments. A blue tint had already taken to the edges of his son's lips and his breathing was too shallow.

"Hold on, Mierta," Mortain urged.

Mierta's breathing has been compromised, but his pulse is still strong. I must act quickly! he thought.

He reached into his robe, grasped Mierta's wand and held it out toward his son. *"Emaculavi el curpas y mehartis!"*

However, the wand would not obey him.

"No, no, no! Don't do this to me! I am not a Magulia, I am a warlock! I studied healing magic at Poveglia. It wasn't my fault. I am a warlock!" Mortain cried, refusing to accept his ability to cast magic had been permanently removed.

Desperate, he placed the wand into his son's hand, forcing him to grip it. He manipulated Mierta's arm to aim the wand over his damaged face and yelled, *"Emaculavi!"*

Again, the wand would not respond.

"Emaculavi!"

After the wand failed to respond a third time, Mortain, disgusted, let Mierta's hand, barely grasping the wand, drop to the bed. He buried his face into the edge of the bed.

A minute later, he came up with another idea and looked up. He calmed himself and glanced over to his son. Everything seemed hopeless, but deep down he believed Mierta would survive. He had to. He was a McKinnon after all, and *there's one thing McKinnon's don't do, and that's give up easily.*

Mortain decided to give his idea a try. "Mierta," he said with urgency. "Listen to me. If you can hear me, open your eyes and take deeper breaths. Mierta?" He could hear the sound of heavy footsteps coming down the hall.

"Here is everything you requested, Monsieur McKinnon," Armand said, entering the bedroom.

"Thank you, Armand," Mortain answered, looking back as Armand placed a bowl and pitcher on the nightstand. "Quickly! Bring the basin closer to the bed."

Once Armand had done so, Mortain gently lifted Mierta from the bed and positioned his head over it.

"Now, pour the water over his hair so we may remove any possible contaminants."

"Oui, Monsieur," Armand replied, lifting the pitcher off the nightstand. As he rinsed Mierta's hair, he became alarmed by the damage to his master's young son's face and thought he no longer looked alive. "Good Monsieur, is the young lord going to be all right? He's awfully pale, and barely breathing."

"I don't know," Mortain answered, shaking his head. He soaked the cloth in the cold water basin and squeezed it, allowing the water to run down his son's face. "His heartbeat is strong, but his breathing is of concern to me. There are burns and swelling in his mouth and throat, preventing him from being able to take deep breaths."

"Will he wake soon?"

"It is doubtful. His body is using all the energy he has left to stay alive. Oh, Armand, what have I done? This is all my fault! As advanced as my son is, he is still just a boy. I should have never left him alone," Mortain muttered, dunking the cloth again.

"Monsieur?"

"Even if he should survive," he explained, squeezing the cloth again over Mierta, "my son's face will never fully heal. He will be scarred for the remainder of his life. I don't know if he will be able to accept that. He is already too burdened. It's not fair. My son, oh my poor boy!"

After fifteen minutes passed, he lifted Mierta again, laid him on the bed and wrapped him in warm blankets. Soaking the cloth once more, he carefully placed it directly over the raw skin.

Mortain then knelt down beside the bed to pray. "My Lord," Mortain said, folding his hands in prayer. Tears forming in his eyes, he looked up and continued, "what have I done to offend thee so? First, you took my magic and then you took my wife. I beseech you! Do not take my son. Don't take him. Please."

"Monsieur McKinnon!" Armand called with urgency, having noticed a change in Mierta's condition.

"Not now Armand," Mortain rejected.

"I beg to differ, Monsieur. Mierta has stopped breathing. I fear he's dying."

"What?" Mortain questioned with disbelief. He gazed over at his son, pulling back the covers for confirmation. Mierta's chest had gone still and his stomach was no longer moving. "Mierta?" He asked in a whisper, tears falling down his face. He leaned in to listen, verifying he could no longer hear air moving.

"No, Mierta," he said, persuading. "It is not your time. Please, son, I beg you, breathe! Breathe! Don't give in."

Mortain gazed up at the ceiling again and held his hands together in prayer. "My Lord, please! He's just a little boy! Spare him!"

Promptly wiping away the tears with his hands, he laid his ear over the centre of Mierta's chest, grateful to hear his son's heart still beating, though it was now fluttering even more rapidly. He lifted his head, and gently laid a hand over Mierta's left breast.

Mortain's mind hastily concluded, *He's still alive, but only just. His face is starting to take on a bluish skin tone. It is only a matter of minutes before I lose my son.*

He stared down at Mierta's body, willing his son to take another breath. Only it remained the same.

"Please, Mierta. Please, son, breathe!" he cried. Then, he began to consult with himself. "What am I missing? Lungs are badly injured, and his throat and mouth are swollen…they must be preventing him from being able to breathe in a lying position. That's it!"

He turned and spoke with authority, "Armand, assist me, quickly! My son must be repositioned before it's too late!"

"Oui, Monsieur McKinnon."

Armand adjusted the pillows on the bed while Mortain carefully lifted his son, so he was in a sitting position.

"Do you believe he is going to be all right now, Monsieur?" Armand questioned, watching Mortain lay a finger on the side of Mierta's neck, checking his pulse.

They both watched Mierta intensely for any changes.

Come on, this has to work! Breathe, Mierta, please! I cannot lose you...

Mortain sighed with relief when he witnessed Mierta start to breathe again on his own, even if it was shallow.

"That, I regret, is yet to be determined," Mortain explained, his face filled with worry. "Mierta must be closely monitored until his lungs heal. There is still a possibility he could stop breathing again or worse, his heart might decide to stop beating. I shall keep vigil and examine him further at first sunlight when I can determine what other treatments may be best for him. The most important thing now is that he be kept quiet and rest."

Armand nodded. "Oui, Monsieur McKinnon. I shall go fetch a nightshirt for the young lord. Please let me know if there's anything else I can do to assist you."

"Thank you, Armand," Mortain answered, smiling graciously.

MIERTA STIRRED when he felt something touch the surface of his lips. It was cold and wet. He tried to open his eyes, but the lids felt heavy and sticky.

"No, Mierta," he heard his father say. "Don't try to open your eyes. You are still very weak. You've been unconscious for two days. Your lips are dry and cracking. I shall give you something to drink, but sip it with caution. Your throat is still very swollen."

Mierta parted his lips slightly and felt a cool wet sensation as his father spooned water into his mouth. The wetness seemed to disappear as soon as it touched his parched tongue. "Mmmmore," he managed to croak out.

A slight smile crossed Mortain's lips as he heard his son speak. "Just a little more, son. Don't want to do too much all at once." He spooned another small portion of water into Mierta's mouth.

This time Mierta could feel the cool water go down his throat. Confusion clouded his mind as it seemed to burn him. He coughed in an attempt to stop the burning.

Mortain crinkled his brow with concern. He set the cup and spoon down on the bedside table. He poured a spoonful of a tincture he had brewed earlier. "It's all right, son. I shall give you something to relieve the pain."

He carefully spooned it into Mierta's mouth and watched as the potion quickly took effect.

"Sleep, my boy. You'll be all right, now."

CHAPTER FIFTEEN

TWO MONTHS LATER...

COINNEACH CASTLE
THE KINGDOM OF VANDOLAY
1238 CE

Orlynd entered the throne room and made his way to Déor. Sunlight shone brightly through a large, round window above the entrance. The sun spot it left on the floor matched its intricate design. Large pillars on either side of the hall stood silently as if they were quietly watching Orlynd approach. Ornate tapestries hung from the tops of the pillars. On the walls behind the pillars were floor-to-ceiling stained glass windows that threw colourful shadows at Orlynd's feet. He looked up to find Déor sitting on the throne with Anya in a chair next to him.

"Orlynd, thank you for coming," Déor said. He stared at Orlynd intently while taking in a deep breath, trying to focus on what he had to say next.

"Is something wrong, Yir Grace?" Orlynd asked, feeling a bit uncomfortable by the king's stare. He pulled his hands together and placed them in the sleeves of his robe.

Déor sighed. "Yes. I never foresaw myself needing to do this, but," he looked over at his queen in the chair beside him, "Anya and I are seeking your counsel."

"Aye, Yir Grace," Orlynd said, a bit surprised.

"There is a matter that has come to my attention. The question is how do I know we can trust you?" Déor inquired.

"Ah'm nae sure Ah understand," Orlynd replied. "Huv Ah done something tae make yis question ma loyalty?"

"If I may?" Anya said, gazing over at Déor.

Déor nodded.

Anya raised an eyebrow. "What I believe my husband is trying to say is that he has more pressing concerns than taking care of this trivial situation, however, he must get involved. There are rumours of brigands poaching the king's fallow deer in Cara Forest, located on the outskirts of the kingdom. It is necessary to confirm these rumours."

"Aye," Déor acknowledged. "Truth is I cannot do this alone, and I won't risk sending just anybody. I have already acquired Aindrias's assistance. He has proven to be more than worthy of completing this task; however, one man may not be enough if we should run into unforeseen trouble."

"Ah'm nae sure Ah follow," Orlynd said.

"I require the aid of your wand. Spells would be more effective than swords against bow and arrows. Can I count on you, Orlynd, to protect us?"

Orlynd swallowed hard. "Aye, Yir Grace. Ah shall wit ma life."

CARA FOREST
THE KINGDOM OF VANDOLAY
1238 CE

CARA FOREST, full of old and young trees, spread across the vast lands to the borders of the kingdoms of Aracelly and Glendalow. The forest was known for the deep red leaves of its trees. Interspersed between the trees were many ferns and flowering plants. The buzz of insects and scurrying of small animals filled the air. Most of the area remained unknown since the thickness of the trees and uneven paths made it difficult to explore. Nevertheless, the forest was the favoured hunting place of the king and his royal hunting party.

"Be on your guard. We do not know what we may find in there," Déor said from his horse. Before proceeding further, he reached into his tunic and pulled out the Bynoch, laying it against his chest.

Noticing the necklace, Orlynd uttered, "Yir Grace is wearing the necklace yir father gave yis."

"Aye. Do you have a problem with that, warlock?" Déor asked with a look of disgust. When Orlynd didn't respond, he said, "I didn't think so."

After following an uneven dirt path with various twists and turns, Déor abruptly stopped and raised his hand in caution when they heard what sounded like an animal's shriek.

"What was that?" Aindrias asked.

"Whitever it wis came fi the west," Orlynd replied.

"Follow me!" Déor grabbed a hold of the reins and urged his horse to gallop faster.

Ten minutes later, the party stopped again when they came upon what looked like blood in the dirt. Déor jumped down from his horse to investigate.

"Animal's blood," he said looking further up the path. "There's a trail." Getting back on his horse, he slowly followed it. He stopped when he noticed the drops getting bigger and closer together. "We are approaching the creature. I suggest we tie our horses off and proceed the rest of the way on foot. Keep an eye on your back. I gather we aren't alone."

The party had only walked up the path a little way when Déor stopped short. He could hear the animal whimpering. Raising his finger to his lips to instruct the others to remain quiet before looking to the right of the path, he saw a patch of brown fur with white stripes and spots. Upon further inspection he concluded it was a fallow deer. By the size of the antlers, it was five- or six-years-old; an arrow protruded from its side. The animal was bleating loudly, and its eyes were wide with fright and pain.

Déor sighed and muttered to the ground as he approached the creature. "It is true, then." He knelt down near the deer's head, withdrew his dagger, and gently lifting the animal's head, he said, "Forgive me. A swift death is a good death." He slit its throat.

All members of the party turned to look when they heard the whooshing of an arrow as it flew past Déor. It landed on the ground beside him.

Déor stared at the arrow before looking up. A few feet away stood a young man dressed in a simple tunic.

Realising he had been seen, Eoghan quickly lowered his bow.

"Brigand!" Déor called out angrily, releasing his sword, Ruairí, from its sheath before charging.

Preston, another brigand, jumped down from a branch in the tree Aindrias was standing beside, stabbing him in the side with his dagger.

"Aindrias!" cried Déor, stopping when he heard his guard cry in pain.

Preston proceeded to kick Aindrias in the stomach, knocking him to the ground.

Gavin, still hiding in another tree, readied his bow and arrow, targeted Déor, and pulled back on the string.

"Gulpe ursígo!" shouted Orlynd as he ran forward towards Déor, knocking the arrow down before it was able to hit the king.

Déor gasped. He glared towards the direction the arrow came from, quickly pulling a star knife from underneath his belt, which he flung at Gavin in an attempt to dislodge him. Déor watched as Gavin tumbled from the tree branch to the ground, his neck pierced.

"Gulpe ursígo!" Orlynd shouted again, startling Déor, in order to protect him against another of Eoghan's arrows. Orlynd quickly raised his wand again. *"Vorbíllion!"*

They watched as Eoghan was sent flying backwards, hitting the ground hard, and appeared to have lost consciousness.

Preston stood over Aindrias, the guard's sword in the brigand's hand, its blade touching the edge of his neck.

Aindrias glanced up into the man's eyes. Preston pressed the blade's edge lightly into Aindrias's neck until there was the beginning of blood. One swing of the sword and everything would be over. There was no hesitation in Preston's face. Aindrias swallowed hard and closed his eyes, ready to admit defeat.

He heard a swish, the sound of blood gushing and something hitting the ground beside him. Aindrias opened his eyes to see Preston's head, which had been sliced from his body with one swing from Déor's sword, lying beside him.

"Come back and face me, you coward!" Déor shouted as Eoghan quickly fled the scene. "You shall hang for this!" He turned. "Aindrias!" exclaimed Déor, turning, noticing the blood soaking through the side of Aindrias's tunic. "You are injured. I am afraid I do not know much about healing practices."

"Do not let it trouble you, Your Grace," Aindrias said between groans. "I have taken worse wounds from a dagger's blade than this. I assure you my life is not in peril."

"I'm relieved. However," Déor said, turning his attention to the warlock, "Orlynd, do you know any spells that can help relieve Aindrias's pain while on the return journey?"

Orlynd shook his head. "Nae, Yir Grace. Ah'm afraid only witches n' warlocks capable ay performing healing magic huv been trained in Poveglia."

"That's unfortunate. Nonetheless, we will have to do our best. Aindrias, will you be able to ride?" Déor asked.

"Yes, Your Grace."

"Allow me tae dress yir wound until we git back tae Vandolay," Orlynd said.

"I was not aware you had the talent to dress wounds," Déor said, watching Orlynd carefully bandage the wound. "Are there other talents you may be hiding from me, warlock?"

"Nae, Yir Grace," Orlynd answered. "Ma father's best mate wis a healer fi Poveglia. Ah believe he taught him some basic techniques, which ma father later taught me."

Déor crossed his arms. "I believe I may have misjudged you, Orlynd. If it hadn't been for what you did back there, all of our lives may have been forfeit. It would appear there is truth to your words. I suggest we make haste for Vandolay, get Aindrias treated, and get some rest."

CHAPTER SIXTEEN

COINNEACH CASTLE
THE KINGDOM OF VANDOLAY
1238 CE

G ood people of the realm, we thank you for your presence on this day in joining us for food and wine. My queen has something she would like to say," Déor spoke with a smile as he turned his attention to his wife. "My queen?"

Anya stood behind a long table, which had been set up for the feast to come. The canopy above waved gently in the light breeze. King Déor and other high members of the court enjoyed the shade it provided. Lesser nobles and their families were seated at tables that had been set up on the grass affording them a sideways view of the main table.

"Thank you, my king," Anya said, turning to those present. "We are so fortunate to be gathered here today to enjoy these privileges, for not all are so fortunate. Today we remember King Francis, the accomplishments and victories he brought to this beloved kingdom and mourn his passing. By royal tradition, we also celebrate the life of his son, Déor, your newly crowned king!" The queen's speech was met with a round of applause and cheers.

Déor smirked, raising his hand to acknowledge his subjects.

"This day marks another important event in the history of our kingdom—the beginning of King Déor's reign. With me, Anya of Glendalow, his queen, at his side, may his reign be long and prosperous! To thank the gods for another year of peace between the kingdoms, the king has decreed all food leftover from the royal hunt will be shared with those in need. Please, join me in raising your cups in a toast to your king! Bring forth the royal goblet!" Anya announced.

From the left end of the table, Orlynd watched the royal goblet holder appear carrying an empty goblet in his hand. From afar it looked like any other golden goblet, but up close the symbol of the family's crest was distinguishable.

Orlynd continued to stare, not showing any kind of happy emotion. He did not mean it as an act of disinterest or disrespect; however, he was finding it difficult to celebrate anything these days. He was still the son of an exiled man, and despite the warning he had delivered to King Francis, Orlynd still felt a remnant of guilt for the king's untimely death. He wondered if Déor felt that way, too? For lately, his cruelty towards Orlynd seemed to have escalated. Nonetheless, it was his sworn duty to serve and protect the king in whatever way he could, even if that meant forfeiting his own life.

The royal goblet holder approached the table, picked up a pitcher, and filled the king's cup to the top. Neither Déor or the goblet holder—or even Orlynd—was aware of the small dab of yellow powder waiting at the bottom of the king's cup. Unaware of what was to come, Déor picked up the cup after the goblet holder had filled it.

"Long live the King!" Anya shouted, raising her cup, gazing over at her husband.

"Long live the King!" the crowd repeated, toasting the King.

Déor grinned before tilting his head back and consuming some of the delicious mead from his goblet, the same recipe preferred by his father. He enjoyed how its essence easily travelled down his throat before it was replaced with a bitter taste. Déor looked down at the cup. He couldn't recall experiencing such a bitter aftertaste before, but he disregarded it and quickly finished the rest.

"Look my dear, the cake!" Anya announced, distracting the king from his thoughts.

Applause sounded from the other attendees. The enormous cake was situated on an oversized tray, which required four sturdy men to carry.

Déor grinned, stood up and released his family's most treasured sword, Ruairí, from its sheath. He walked around the table and approached the cake. The cake bearers prayed the king wouldn't accidentally miss his mark and slice one of them instead.

The king raised a hand to acknowledge the crowd before raising his sword to deliver a fatal blow to the cake. However, he forthwith dropped his sword, causing the crowd to gasp in surprise.

The king's eyes grew wide. He coughed, feeling an intense sensation of dryness and burning fill his mouth. He attempted to swallow, only to find it difficult as he reached up a hand to his throat.

This was different than the last time a member of the royal family had been suspected of ingesting poison. In fact, Mortain had informed the court that Francis had succumbed from a sudden illness.

"Your Grace?" one of the cake bearers asked, alarmed to see the king's face looking as red as a tomato.

Orlynd stood up at the table, sensing trouble, when Déor stood frozen.

"Water," he said, between coughs, his voice sounding hoarse. "Fetch water!"

"Yis heard the man, git him some water! Now!" Orlynd shouted at the royal goblet holder, running from around his side of the table to the king's aid.

The goblet holder raced to grab the king's goblet, filling it with water from a pitcher on another table, before bringing it back to the king.

The king nodded between coughs, no longer able to acknowledge his royal goblet holder with words, tilted his head back and attempted to consume the water. Eyes growing wider, he realised his ability to swallow had been halted. Thinking quickly, he vomited out what was left in his mouth, most of it ending up on the grass in front of him. The choking coughs started again.

"He cannae breathe!" Orlynd announced, the gasps from the spectators becoming louder.

Everyone watched in horror as the king fell to his knees. Orlynd hurried forward, wrapping his arms around him as support, helping him lie on the ground.

"Yir Majesty, hold oan!" Orlynd exclaimed; the fear in the king's eyes matched his own. He watched as the king's normally rugged tone turned bluish-grey. The whites of his eyes had already become a faint red. Orlynd looked to the crowd and shouted. "Someone fetch the court physician!"

Without warning, Orlynd felt the king's body twitch, followed by stillness. He watched blood begin to drip profusely from the corner of the king's mouth.

"Yer Majesty?" Orlynd said. He placed a hand over Déor's chest and gasped when he could no longer feel a heartbeat. "Nae." He laid the king on the ground, stood up and addressed everyone. "The king's dead. He has been poisoned, murdered, jist like his father! N Ah will nae rest until thair killer meets their end!"

Anya stood back in the shadows unseen, a small smile curving her lips as she saw her plan unfolding before her eyes.

ORLYND'S COTTAGE
THE KINGDOM OF VANDOLAY
1238 CE

ORLYND GASPED, quickly opening his eyes, and found himself back in bed. His breathing was rapid, his heart was racing, and his brow was moist from sweat. He looked around, realising he was in what could be best described as a servant's room. He permitted his body to relax.

Whit a terrible dream, Orlynd thought to himself. He had numerous nightmares before, but never anything as intense as that.

Rubbing his hands over his face, he decided to stand up and wet his face with a cloth. He walked to a small mirror positioned on top of the dresser and stared at his reflection. He caught a glimpse of the remnants of flames in the pupils of his eyes. His eyes widened, realising what he had just seen was a vision of a gathering scheduled for later in the week. "It wasn't a nightmare; it was a premonition!"

Nae, this cannae be. Ah cannae allow this event tae occur. Ah must find a ain tae stop it!

CHAPTER SEVENTEEN

COINNEACH CASTLE
THE KINGDOM OF VANDOLAY
1238 CE

LONG LIVE the King!" toasted the crowd to King Déor's lengthy reign, two months exactly since his father's passing.

Déor grinned before tilting his head back and consuming some of the delicious mead in his goblet.

Queen Anya smiled, anticipating when Déor would become ill. However, minutes past and nothing happened.

Once Déor set the goblet down, he looked over and noticed Orlynd had not taken the toast to his celebration and was staring intently at the goblet.

"My love? Are you feeling all right?" questioned Anya, puzzled as to how her plan had failed. She would see to it later that the guard she bribed would be involved in some type of accident, which would result in his life being lost, as punishment for disobeying her orders.

"Aye, I'm fine," Déor answered, distracted. He took in a deep breath, hoping to not have to show his authoritative figure by punishing the warlock. This was a time for celebration, not a time to dole out punishment. The thought only served to anger him even more. He clenched a fist and leaned in towards the warlock.

"Are you deliberately trying to embarrass me in front of my queen and our people?"

Orlynd startled. "Nae, Yir Grace. Ah am nae thirsty," Orlynd replied uneasily. Based on his recent vision, whoever had succeeded in taking the late king's life was still in court. In fact, he or she was probably mingled in between all the guests today. He had been carefully checking various cups before the day's event, but all of the goblets had the appearance of the same golden colour. The only distinguishable feature of the king's goblet was the symbol of the family's crest, which could only be seen from the inside when empty or half filled with liquid. Orlynd had managed to substitute it with his own goblet when no one was looking.

"You're not thirsty?" replied Déor with a sneer. He turned back to Anya. "Can you believe this nonsense?"

The queen played along by raising an eyebrow and chuckling.

Déor returned his gaze to the warlock. "You will drink to my honour!"

"Ah beg ay yis, Yir Grace. Dinnae make me drink. If yis dae, Ah will nae be able tae perform ma duty," Orlynd answered. He could feel his heart pounding in his ears and sweat starting to form on his brow. There was no point in revealing to Déor the real reason he didn't wish to drink the mead. Déor wouldn't have believed him anyway.

Déor clenched a fist, trying to hold back his anger. How long would it be before any of the other guests noticed Orlynd's behaviour? And his queen? She was sitting there right next to him. Would she think he was unworthy to be king if he didn't discipline his soothsayer? He concluded he had no other choice.

Déor stood from his chair and stood in front of Orlynd. "Ladies and gentlemen, my soothsayer has refused to drink to my honour. He's afraid of becoming tipsy!"

A mischievous grin formed on his face as he slowly paced alongside the long wooden table, listening to the crowd laugh.

"What say you? What shall I do to resolve this? Should I send him to spend the night in the dungeons of Tarloch Castle?" He smirked at the response of a couple of cheers from the audience. "Or, perhaps I should send him to the stocks?" He waited again for the crowd's response.

Orlynd stared at him, blood rushing to his face. He had received more than his fair share of cruelty because he had been born an O'Brien. He could never go outside the castle's walls without being stared at, taunted, or having something thrown at him. In his heart he felt he would never be rid of this shame; however, it was obvious Déor was more than enjoying himself at his expense.

"Nae. I have decided. Royal goblet holder," he called, pointing, "fill this warlock's goblet to the top! He shall consume all the liquid until I am able to see the bottom of his goblet."

Orlynd focused intently on the goblet as the royal goblet holder obeyed. This wasn't how it was supposed to end. His Rite of Wands had distinctly showed him war would be coming to the Kingdom of Vandolay.

He would be there, standing in the middle of the field outside of the castle's walls, which would be transformed into a battlefield overnight. Spilled blood and dead bodies mixed in the overgrown grass, and the sound of swords clashing against each other could be heard in the distance. He could see Déor, who had just cut down a soldier with his family's sword, about a hundred feet in front of him on horseback.

Without warning, Orlynd heard the cry of the banshee. In that precise moment, he watched Déor fall from his horse. Déor grimaced in pain, placing his hand over his stomach where an injury had taken place. Orlynd shouted His Highness's name and raced to his aid. Then everything had gone dark.

Orlynd was aware that fates could be changed, and it was obvious his had. He would never get to see whether or not Déor would become a "good" king as he had hoped he would. If the events of his Rite of Wands should become reality, and the king should fall in battle like he had seen, he would not be there to help him.

Orlynd wondered if his own death would be swift, or if it would be painful. It wasn't that he was afraid of dying. It was the process of getting there that scared him.

His mind then reflected on Francis's dead body. He recalled seeing a metallic liquid dripping from his mouth, but there had been no doubt that he had passed. Would the same thing happen to him, too? Certainly, once he was dead, everyone would believe he had been the one who poisoned King Francis. Until the real murderer succeeded in killing again.

Orlynd stood from his chair once the goblet had been slammed down in front of him. He grasped it in his hand. His heart had already picked up its pace. Maybe, there was a slight chance at earning redemption for his family by sacrificing himself for the King. He looked up at Déor.

Déor gazed back, a smug expression on his face.

Orlynd swallowed hard. "May yir reign be long n fulfilling," he stated. "Ah pray yis find the balance between confidence n humility. God save the King!"

Instead of being overly pleased, Déor became perplexed by Orlynd's profound statement. He watched the warlock raise the goblet to his lips and gulp the concoction.

At first, Orlynd felt the gorse flower dry mead that finished with the sweet taste of honey, coconut and vanilla gently travel down his throat. Shortly afterward, the taste was replaced by something bitter and acrid.

Orlynd set the empty goblet on the table. Abruptly, an intense sensation of dryness and burning of his mouth overcame him. He grimaced when he attempted to swallow, finding it suddenly difficult.

Déor studied Orlynd's face, seeing the beginnings of a rash appear.

Anya was also staring, trying her best to hide the rage building up inside her.

Orlynd, the fool! He has consumed the poison meant for the king! she thought.

On the other hand, the queen deduced, with the elimination of the king's soothsayer, it would become easier for her to carry out her plan to kill Déor. A small grin crept to her mouth.

"What's the matter with you? Why didn't you inform me you were allergic to mead?" Déor inquired.

Orlynd wanted to explain to him, but instead his mind begged him to relieve the sensation of thirst.

Tears filled Orlynd's eyes. "Burning. Water...need water," he whispered. He raced over to where a large jug of water was positioned on a guest's table.

"Where are you going? Orlynd? Orlynd! I command you to get back here!" Déor shouted.

Instead of pouring the water into another glass, Orlynd lifted the container and tilted it until water hit his mouth. However, when he tried to swallow, he couldn't, and he began to cough up the little bit of water he was able to ingest, spilling the remainder of the water down the front of his robe.

The spectators gasped.

Déor was shocked. He had never seen Orlynd behave this way.

Has he gone mad? Déor thought. *How dare he embarrass me in front of my guests!* He then recalled the last thing Orlynd had said to him.

"Ah pray yis find the balance between confidence n humility." Was he insinuating he was missing something important?

His thoughts were quickly distracted by the sound of Orlynd screaming.

Déor blinked.

Orlynd collapsed to his knees, his hands desperately trying to find his face. He swung his arms around like someone who had had hot coals thrown in their face.

"Orlynd?" Déor said with concern.

Déor quickly turned and examined the goblet Orlynd had drunk from, lifting it toward his face. It was at that moment he noticed the small crest shining from the bottom of the goblet. His eyes widened, and his blood ran cold.

This is my goblet. My goblet was switched with his. How can this be?

His thoughts again became distracted by the sound of Orlynd's continued screaming. "Ah can't..."

Shock displayed on Déor's face. Chaos had ignited. The spectators, instead of helping the warlock, were running away from him in fear of catching whatever ailed him.

"Please, everyone," Déor stated, his voice quivering. "Stay where you are and do not panic."

However, no one was listening.

What have I done? Orlynd was trying to warn me. He must have known I would not have listened to any of his excuses. What kind of king am I? I have sent my father's advisor to his death. Is this an omen of my reign?

Anya stood from her chair. "Déor, do something about this. Get rid of him before he ruins your day of celebration!"

The king watched the warlock lose consciousness and collapse onto the ground.

"The celebration is already over," he whispered, acknowledging the empty tables once filled with guests. He stepped down from the raised wooden platform and rushed to Orlynd's side. "Orlynd?" he asked, his fingers trembling. "Please, do not be dead."

Déor started to reach out a hand to check for a pulse when he noticed the frantic twitching vein in the warlock's neck. The poison which had made Orlynd so ill had already reached his heart and was continuing to quickly circulate throughout the remainder of his body.

"How is he?" Anya inquired, having left her place at the table to join her husband.

Orlynd. Why? Why would you sacrifice yourself for me? Déor contemplated.

"Your Majesty?"

"Orlynd's life is in peril. Someone deliberately slipped poison in his goblet," Déor answered. He began to stand up. "We can delay no further. His heart is beating too fast. Please, have the court physician summoned here immediately."

"That will not be possible," Anya answered.

"Why not? I am the King."

"Because a pigeon arrived with a letter from Glendalow a fort-night ago," Anya interrupted, shock displaying over Déor's face to the announcement. "Mortain requested our forgiveness and sent his regrets that he would be unable to attend our coronation due to his son, Mierta, having been involved in some sort of potion accident."

"What?" Déor cried, raising his hand in the air and clenched it. "Why wasn't I told?" He lowered his hand and quickly regathered his thoughts. He turned to a nearby servant. "Send a pigeon back to the McKinnon Estate. In the name of the King, I order Mortain to return to Vandolay to treat my soothsayer. Tell him it is urgent. He may think because I am now King, he can put aside his duties. Assign a carriage to escort him back to the castle, and instruct him to meet me in my private apartment. I shall take Orlynd there personally to avoid any further commotion. In the meantime, send a messenger to seek out the most talented Apothecarist in the kingdom. I have heard my father speak of one located in this area, but I do not know how to reach him for I do not know his name. I will not permit my warlock to die because my court physician decided to take a holiday."

"I will send them immediately," the servant answered.

Anya carefully eyed the warlock from behind Déor. Slipping in a smirk, she took her leave.

Déor carefully repositioned Orlynd onto his back and gasped at what he saw.

Orlynd's face had gone beet red. The rash had become more distinguishable and had spread across the front of his neck and upper torso. His mouth was partially open, and his breathing was rapid and uneasy.

Déor placed a hand over Orlynd's chest in order to provide what little comfort he could, feeling intense heat coming through the robe and the frantic thumping of Orlynd's heart.

"Hold on, Orlynd," he said. "As your King, I am commanding you to live." He lifted Orlynd, cradling the warlock's body near his chest. Orlynd's arms hung limply from his body. *"Guards!"* shouted Déor.

One of the king's guards appeared right away, after brushing aside some curtains.

"Your Majesty?" he said, bowing before Déor. "Allow me to assist you by carrying the warlock." He reached out for Orlynd.

"Nay," Déor said. "Thank you, Thomas, but Orlynd's fate is my responsibility. However, there is another matter I need your assistance with."

"Anything, Your Grace," Thomas replied.

"Arrest my royal goblet holder for his failed attempt to poison his king!" Déor said. "Do whatever you need to do in order to get him to confess."

"Yes, sire," Thomas answered a bit uneasily, shock displayed on his face.

Déor started to walk away but stopped. "And when you're finished send another pigeon to the McKinnon Estate. I want to see for myself the result of this potion accident. Summon Mierta."

CHAPTER EIGHTEEN

MCKINNON ESTATE
GLENDALOW
1238 CE

"All right, now, take in a slow deep breath," Mortain instructed his son for what seemed like the thousandth time since Mierta first woke from his accident. "Go on, then."

Mierta pursed his lips and inhaled, feeling the tiniest bit lightheaded but overall the best he had felt in two weeks.

"Good," answered Mortain, listening, pleased to hear everything flowing smoothly. "Now release it." He was not pleased, however, when he heard the sound of multiple heaving coughs. "Well, that was unfortunate," Mortain frowned, continuing his observation, "but not unexpected. Your lungs are still healing after all. It will take some time."

"Time? I don't have time! We're wasting it!" Mierta complained between wheezing breaths. He had to create a cure before the plague he had seen in his Rite of Wands hit. He felt his father place an arm around him, guiding him back over to his bed, forcing him to take a seat. He was certain he would never fully embrace his heart feeling like it wanted to explode inside his chest.

"Now, now, I understand your fear, son, but it is best that you rest. Unnecessary exertion would be ill-advised."

"But all I ever do anymore is rest!" Mierta protested. "It's not fair. I'm tired of resting! It has been weeks! It's boring. Certainly, it must have been long enough?"

"Mierta, must I remind you, you have been very ill? You will be of no help to me by jeopardising your own health," Mortain said, attempting to convince him.

"Father, I'm fine," Mierta retorted.

"My son, you are not fine," Mortain replied. "Your lungs and throat were so injured that it was only by God's good grace that you survived at all. I know you are eager to try to hone your skill at compounding chemicals, but if recent events have proven anything, it is that you are not ready."

"What? But, Father!"

"I do not expect you to understand, but I'm requesting you try. The fault is not yours. You are, after all, still very young. No, I admit the fault is mine. The act of compounding chemicals is a delicate matter and should not be done unsupervised. I will forever regret my decision, for the repercussions are irreversible and nearly cost you your life."

"Father, please," Mierta begged, tears forming in his eyes. "Do not blame yourself. It was an accident. It was *my* accident! I went looking through the book believing I could find a recipe I could compound on my own. I thought I could make you proud."

I am proud of you; you are my son, Mortain thought.

"Instead I have brought shame and embarrassment to the family," Mierta continued.

No, Mierta…

"I am sorry. I'm so sorry!" Mierta said, looking up, his face full of guilt and regret. "Please, I beg you, do not prevent me from discovering the one thing that I must."

Mortain looked away. He could not bear to look into his son's face when he uttered the next words, "I'm sorry, my son, but I cannot permit you to continue practicing compounding chemicals until you are of the proper age. I cannot risk the possibility of losing you again." He turned back to his son. "You will obey me, will you not?"

Mierta bowed his head in defeat. "Yes, Father," he responded, his voice breaking.

"Thank you, Son," Mortain answered, relieved. "Now, lay your head back down on the pillow. I need to replace your bandage."

Mierta nodded and did as his father asked, blinking back tears, determined not to show any weakness even though he felt like his heart was breaking in two. His resolve failed the moment his father pulled a chair over to the bed and started to pull the bandage away from his face.

Listening to his son sniffing, watching him wipe away tears, Mortain furrowed his brow, trying to hide his worry. He hated hurting his son like this. He felt if his heart could break, it would at that very instant. Mierta was ready, he never doubted it. The fact that he had even attempted to make a potion solidified that he was. However, he reflected with sadness, being able to successfully compound chemicals did not guarantee prosperity. He had to protect his son, and if the only way to prevent Mierta from making the same grave mistakes he did was to forbid him, then Mortain was prepared to do so. Perhaps then Mierta would give up compounding altogether.

As he gently pulled away the bandage, veins could be seen where thick scar tissue had already formed. He was pleased to see the salve he had been placing on Mierta's face since the accident had both soothed and aided in the healing process, though he doubted he would see any further improvement.

"How does it look?" Mierta asked. He didn't wish to have half of his face damaged for the rest of his life, but it was a punishment he would accept. He began questioning whether being an Apothecarist really was his fate.

"It is healing, as expected," Mortain said, handing Mierta a small bowl of salve after helping his son sit back up. "This emollient will help soothe the pain from the burns and nerve damage. And if you must step outside, it is of the utmost importance you cover your face with the bandages I have left in your nightstand."

"Yes, Father," Mierta answered.

"Monsieur McKinnon! Monsieur McKinnon!" shouted Armand, his quick footsteps echoing against the wooden floor as he ran up a flight of stairs and down the hallway. He stopped at the doorframe of Mierta's room breathing heavily, sweat starting to drip down his brow.

Mortain turned his head. "Armand, what on God's good earth is the matter?"

"I'm sorry, Monsieur," Armand answered between heavy breaths. "A pigeon just arrived with this letter. It's from the Kingdom of Van-dolay from the king and queen.'"

"Bring it to me," Mortain instructed, taking the paper from Armand's hands. He opened it and quickly read over the message.

"No," Mortain whispered, his face going pale.

Hearing the shock in his father's voice, Mierta grew concerned. "Father, what is it? What's wrong? Has something happened to the King?"

Not Orlynd, not my good mate's son. Please, by God's good grace, let this be a mistake!

"Monsieur, are you all right?"

Mortain lowered the letter, folding it in his hands. "I must prepare to leave. The king's young soothsayer has been taken seriously ill, and I must tend to him," Mortain answered matter-of-factly, quickly standing up to start preparing for the journey.

Even if I leave now, I will never make it. It's hopeless! Orlynd, hold on!

"His Majesty is sending a carriage, but time is not to be wasted. I shall go by horse and meet the carriage." He stopped when he heard Lochlann crying from his crib. "Oh, good gracious." His voice was full of anxiety. "Armand, please fetch Natasha and have her tend to him."

"Oui, Monsieur," Armand replied, leaving the room.

"Mierta, hand me back the key to the cellar."

"What? Why? Can't I come with you?" Mierta said, standing up. "You promised me an apprenticeship!"

Mortain turned back. "Yes, I did, Mierta, but this is not the time or the place to discuss it."

"So, that's how it's going to be then, is it? You're going back on your word," Mierta accused.

Mortain sighed. "Mierta, you are too young to understand. I promise to explain everything to you, after I return, all right? Hand me the key, please."

With heavy steps, Mierta stomped over to his dresser, removed the key and threw it onto the floor in front of his father's feet.

"Mierta!" Mortain scolded. "Whatever has gotten into you? Pick up that key this instant!"

"No! You lied to me!" Mierta alleged. "You never wanted me to have an apprenticeship."

"Now, be fair. You know that is not true. I understand you are upset, son, but you must understand."

"You promised me an apprenticeship," Mierta interrupted, tears forming in his eyes. "Why would you lie to me?"

Baffled by his son's reaction, he eyed him carefully. "Mierta, listen, I haven't. You still will get an apprenticeship. But right now is not the time. Any delay will jeopardise Orlynd's life." He could see his son's body trembling, and Mierta's breathing had become rapid and shallow again. He could clearly hear the sound of his lungs whistling. Their discussion about the apprenticeship would have to wait.

"Mierta," his voice getting anxious. "I need you to slow your breathing and calm yourself. You are making yourself ill again."

"I...I...I can't," he mouthed between a series of harsh coughs. He leaned over, gasping, trying to catch his breath. He could feel blood rushing to his head and his heart pounding from the exertion. As his eyes watered involuntarily, Mierta feared his lungs were going to close on him again.

Placing his hands on his knees, Mierta willed his breathing to slow. With each intake of breath, he was able to breathe a little deeper. After about a minute his breathing had returned almost to normal.

"Monsieur McKinnon! Monsieur McKinnon!" Mortain could hear Armand running up the stairs again.

"What is it this time, Armand? Can you not see I am engaged in trying to help my son?"

"Oui, Monsieur, my apologies. That's why I came back so quickly to see you. Another pigeon has delivered a letter. It's for Mierta. I read it over, sir, and there's no mistake of it. He's been summoned, too."

"What? This is preposterous! I will never forgive the king for this."

"What?" Mierta tried to ask, between coughs. "What's wrong?"

Mortain turned back to stare into Mierta's confused face. "It would appear the king doubts your condition, my son," he said, placing the letter in Mierta's lap. "You have been summoned to court by the King of Vandolay. Any misgivings His Majesty may have shall be proven for naught. While I do not feel it is safe for you to travel, you have been summoned, therefore must appear."

CHAPTER NINETEEN

COINNEACH CASTLE
THE KINGDOM OF VANDOLAY
1238 CE

What is taking so long?" Déor uttered impatiently, pacing back and forth. He had taken Orlynd to the blue bedroom, named after the colour of the painted walls, located directly behind the drawing room of his private apartment.

Déor laid the warlock on the bed and helped loosen Orlynd's robe. He pulled back the blue sheets and stopped, distracted by the sound of Orlynd's breathing as his chest rose and fell rapidly, yet shallowly. Orlynd's condition was quickly declining and there was little he could do.

"A king should not be kept waiting," Déor spoke, slamming his hands against the edge of the bed.

He started pacing the length of the ornately carved mahogany bed. The thick woven rug that covered most of the wood floor was soft under his feet. Déor stopped pacing briefly and stared blankly at the picture of the large landscape of his gardens on the wall just above the bed's headboard, while a slight breeze from the open window at the end of the room blew in his face. He felt haunted by thoughts of his recent poor decisions.

The sound of his guard's voice brought him back to the present.

"Please, Your Grace must not worry so. I'm confident the healer will arrive soon," Aindrias answered, trying his best to calm and counsel his king, though he questioned his own confidence.

"Time is not on our side, Aindrias! Orlynd is getting worse." Déor felt helpless, watching his advisor fade before him. Convincing himself of Orlynd's fate, Déor stated, "Thomas has failed me."

"I beg to differ. We do not know that," Aindrias replied.

Déor paced back and forth again, before stopping. "Do not patronise me. We do know that! My court physician will not arrive in time to aid me. Orlynd's death will not be swift or painless. He shall suffer greatly, and the blame is mine. I do not wish for his forgiveness, for I shall never forgive myself. Ever since Orlynd's arrival, I have been nothing but cruel to him. I never permitted myself to earn his friendship, yet he willingly offered his life for mine. Tell me, Aindrias, why would he do that?"

"Because it is his duty to protect you, as it is mine, Your Grace," Aindrias answered.

"Yes, but I am not his king. He is a citizen of the Kingdom of Aracelly. The dragon, Lord is their ruler, not Déor of Vandolay," Déor replied. He brought a chair near the bed and sat down, glancing at Orlynd, his eyes filled with worry. He took hold of Orlynd's left hand and was alarmed by the heat he felt coming off it. "His fever has increased." He stood up again and felt Orlynd's brow. Alarmed, he turned towards Aindrias. "His skin is dry. He should be sweating out the poison, but instead, it is as if he's being sucked dry from the inside. Why isn't he sweating?"

Aindrias did not respond, his own mind lost for words.

"Is this my punishment, Aindrias?" Déor sounded exasperated as he spoke. "Am I to watch the warlock die for my insensitivity? If so, I beg the gods to grant me my wish and spare Orlynd's life and take mine instead. I can change. Nay, I will change. I will become a good king, a king that will be loved by all of his people, just like my father was. Orlynd did nothing to displease me. He was only obeying what I commanded him to do." Déor closed his eyes and prayed.

An abrupt sound of the door to the private apartment being swung open interrupted Déor's thoughts.

Déor looked back with a tear in his eye.

Thomas bowed. "Please forgive the intrusion, Your Majesty. I have brought the man you have been searching for."

Déor breathed a sigh of relief, his heart warming. "Thank you, Thomas. Please, let him in right away," Déor said, standing from his chair.

An attractive man with fair skin and long, dark brown hair entered and bowed before the king. He carried himself with an air of self-importance with his head held high. The long, black tunic he wore stretched from his squared shoulders to his feet. He held the orange coloured cape at his waist so it would not distract from his presence. When Déor eyed him over, he got the feeling that this man felt everyone should notice him, not his clothing.

"Thank you, Thomas. You may leave us, but please watch at the door," Déor said.

"Yes, Your Grace," Thomas answered, bowing, before taking his leave.

Déor waited until the door was closed before turning his attention back to the man. "Are you the Apothecarist my father spoke of who studied in Edesia and taught lessons?" he said. "You may speak freely."

"I am," he replied with a self-important smirk.

Déor smiled, relieved. "Thank the good Lord. I was beginning to doubt my messenger had reached you."

The man smiled slyly. "I shall work on finding a better hiding place next time, Your Grace."

Déor already disliked this man's arrogance. "What name do you go by?"

"Ezekiel Kavanagh at your service, Your Grace," Ezekiel answered matter-of-factly, clearing his throat. "I understand someone in court has become seriously ill. Please, show me where the patient is."

Déor nodded. He led Ezekiel over to the bed. "It is my advisor, the warlock, Orlynd. It is my belief he consumed mead that was poisoned, at the celebration of my coronation," he said. "I suspect Orlynd somehow found out about it and switched his goblet with mine."

"I see," Ezekiel replied, listening intently. When he reached the bed, the first thing he noticed were blisters that had started to form over Orlynd's face. They looked like they desperately wanted to explode. He also took note of Orlynd's uneven breathing.

Ezekiel calmly placed a finger over the side of Orlynd's neck.

"Please," Déor spoke with a voice full of anxiety, interrupting Ezekiel's examination. "I beg you. Tell me you can save him."

Ezekiel eyed Déor before focusing on what he needed to do next. It was obvious he could not allow Orlynd to die. The king could punish him severely for that. Given the advanced state of the warlock's condition, Ezekiel wasn't sure there was any cure. Nevertheless, he was determined to find a solution. Ezekiel lifted his head.

"If I am to save the warlock's life, it is necessary to determine what specifically made him ill. I require the goblet he drank from," he spoke calmly.

Déor nodded, handing the goblet to him.

Ezekiel raised the goblet to his nose and sniffed it, not smelling anything out of the ordinary. Next, he glimpsed inside the goblet, at first seeing nothing, but on a second, deeper observation, he noticed remnants of a yellowish powder at the bottom of the goblet.

"You are correct in your assessment. Orlynd has been poisoned. He consumed *Atropa belladonna var lutea*."

"Excuse me, what?"

Ezekiel smirked. He loved when he had the opportunity to speak medical verbiage. It made him look smart. "Nightshade," he replied.

"Oh," Déor's heart dropped. "I'm certain he has drunk our mead before. Wouldn't he have been able detect it?"

"No, he would have only been able to taste mead. However, *Atropa belladonna var lutea* is swift. He would have soon become overwhelmed by an acid burning in his mouth and throat. Most people think it's a good idea to attempt to wash it down with water, only to discover they can't."

"That's what happened to Orlynd," Déor murmured.

"Indeed," Ezekiel responded. He leaned forward and gently lifted Orlynd's eyelids. Scanning over his brown eyes, Ezekiel became displeased. "His pupils are dilated. He has lost the ability to accommodate to the changing light. Do you recall if he experienced confusion or trouble seeing?"

"Yes," Déor answered, finding it hard to forget Orlynd's screaming. He was beginning to feel even more regret.

"His temperature is dangerously high," Ezekiel stated, after laying a hand over Orlynd's brow. "Your Grace, I urge you to command your servants to gather all the linens they can find. I must apply wet towels to the warlock's body in order to lower his temperature. If that should fail, I will obtain leeches to draw the fever out."

"It shall be done," Déor confirmed. He turned towards the door of his private apartment and shouted, "Thomas!"

The sound of Thomas's armour clanking against the wooden floor was heard as he approached.

"Your Grace," Thomas said, bowing.

"Instruct the servants to seek out all the linens they can find and bring them here."

"Yes, sire," Thomas answered, before scuttling out of the room.

The king anxiously turned back to Ezekiel, who was cradling Orlynd's left hand while placing his ear over the centre of Orlynd's chest. "Is it too late to save him?"

Ezekiel lifted his head. "Orlynd's fate is grim. The poison has already attacked his respiratory and circulatory systems. His heart is being forced to contract harder and faster to compensate for his shallow breathing, and I can do nothing to assist it," Ezekiel glanced down momentarily towards the bed. "I shall require a visit to my Apothecary to retrieve a tincture from the Calabar bean, which will help to slow his pulse and reverse the spread of the poison. The next twenty-four hours are critical. If he should make it through the night, I'm confident he will recover. However, it is recommended to prepare arrangements."

"Preparing arrangements for what, Ezekiel? I demand an explanation."

Ezekiel stared at Déor, not feeling the need to answer him.

"No! That will not happen. Orlynd will survive this. He has to."

Ezekiel briefly lifted his eyebrows, a bit surprised by Déor's reaction. He cleared his throat again. "There is one other thing you can do to help him."

"What is it? Whatever it is I will do it!" Déor said.

"The warlock needs to be undressed and his body cooled. Once the linens arrive, prepare a large basin of water, dunk the linens into it and lay them over him. Be cautious. He may experience a fit if his temperature is lowered too quickly. I shall return shortly."

"Thank you for your kindness," Déor replied.

"Anytime," Ezekiel smirked before bowing and taking his leave.

Déor turned his attention back to the warlock. "Hold on, Orlynd. Please, stay with me."

CHAPTER TWENTY

COINNEACH CASTLE
THE KINGDOM OF VANDOLAY
1238 CE

Y our Grace!" Mortain exclaimed, barging into the private apartment with Mierta following behind him, "We came as quickly as we could."

Unexpectedly, he stopped walking when he noticed Ezekiel leaning over, finishing an administration of a small tincture to Orlynd. The warlock was still lying in bed, covered only by bed sheets, his chest rising and falling at an even pace for the first time since he had become so ill. It had been two days since the warlock's initial poisoning, and he still had not woken.

Ezekiel picked his head up and pursed his mouth in a self-satisfied smirk. "Good afternoon. I am Ezekiel Kavanagh, at your service. His Grace has gone to rest. I take it you have interest in this patient?"

Mortain smiled politely. "Yes. I am His Grace's court physician."

"Is that so? I do beg your pardon, you are Mortain McKinnon, are you not? Your reputation precedes you."

Mortain's cheeks blushed. "Yes. Why, thank you."

"And you must be his son, Mierta," Ezekiel stated matter-of-factly, noticing the large bandage covering Mierta's left cheek. He raised an eyebrow. "Shame you had such an unfortunate accident with compounding chemicals. Hearing the tale of your circumstances sent His Grace into a bit of a frenzy." He laughed.

"I didn't mean to cause any trouble," Mierta replied, frowning, raising his hand to his mouth to cover a cough.

"Now, now, that is enough small chat, yes? How is the warlock?" Mortain intervened, not wanting Mierta to be further upset.

Ezekiel eyed Mortain, before turning his attention back to Orlynd, pretending to ignore Mortain. "The warlock is not fully recovered yet. I'll admit when I first encountered the boy, I did not expect him to survive, but he has a remarkable resilience about him."

"That is wonderful news indeed," Mortain smiled.

"Yes," Ezekiel replied, turning his head and staring at Mierta before speaking again. "I imagine your son inherited his talents from his father." Ezekiel lifted the goblet, sitting on a nightstand untouched since the original incident. "Mierta, please examine the inside of the goblet. Tell me, what can you distinguish about the poison that was ailing Orlynd? Does the goblet in particular have an unusual odour? Be quick!"

Mierta glimpsed over the goblet with uncertainty. What if he was unable to come up with the answer? He hated the idea of embarrassing his father, but he also felt compelled to prove he was ready for compounding. He raised the goblet to his nose. A very faint fruity fragrance with a mix of honey suckle, coconut and vanilla filled his nostrils—the three key ingredients to the king's favourite mead. However, the remnants of the poison were completely hidden.

"There's nothing unusual about the fragrance. It just smells like mead," Mierta reported.

"That's correct. Well done." Ezekiel smiled. "The culprit is concealed to the human nose. The warlock would have had no knowledge that what he was about to drink was poison. Now, please, look back inside the goblet. Do you notice anything that should not be present, but is?"

Mierta took a deep breath before inspecting the inside of the goblet. At first, he noticed nothing out of the ordinary, taking note of the crest of the kingdom embedded into the goblet. Then his eyes grew wide and his pulse increased when he noticed remnants of a yellowish-green substance at the bottom. "Yes," Mierta answered, looking up at his father. "I reckon I have seen this before. It is some kind of flower or berry."

"That is correct. It is the yellow flowered form of deadly nightshade. It originates from a perennial herbaceous plant in the tomato family. Mortain, may I inquire about your plans for your son's future?"

"Yes, well," Mortain began, proud of Mierta's ability to pass Ezekiel's challenge. "I would imagine it would only be advisable his father teaches him all that he knows when he is of age."

"I see," Ezekiel said, fixed on Mierta. "And may I ask when will that be exactly? Your son is very advanced for his age and should expect nothing but the best education."

"And who would you suggest teach him?" Mortain retorted, feeling defensive.

"I will train the boy. I admit his limited knowledge has impressed me, Mortain. I will arrange living quarters, food and clothing for him at no trouble to you. I will also provide him a quill, paper and a pigeon by which means he can write. I will release him when I feel his skill is satisfactory, and I will not accept no for an answer. You should expect him to do great things, Mortain."

"That is very kind of you," Mortain replied, indignantly, "but I don't know."

Disregarding Mortain's comment, Ezekiel again addressed Mierta. "That cough of yours, that is a result of your accident, no? I have some medicine at my Apothecary which will help with that and promote further healing of your lungs. Come by and see me later. I do not expect I will be needed here much longer, now that His Grace's court physician has arrived," he finished, turning to Mortain with a smirk. "I leave him in your good care. I bid a good day to you all."

CHAPTER TWENTY-ONE

COINNEACH CASTLE
THE KINGDOM OF VANDOLAY
1238 CE

T he next morning, the sun shined brightly through the window of the king's private apartment. The sound of birds singing echoed through the room.

Déor opened his eyes and wiped the sleep out of them. He stretched and stood up from the chair he had fallen asleep in the night before. He tilted his head slightly, thinking he heard something when he realised he could hear Orlynd speaking, though it sounded breathy and weak, like a whisper. "Orlynd is speaking," he said, breathing in and out. "Everyone, wake up right now!"

The announcement woke both Mierta and Mortain who had also fallen asleep in chairs.

Déor, torn between intense excitement and worry, gazed quickly over towards the bed. He confirmed he could hear the warlock speaking. "What are you saying?" he whispered. He turned to Mortain. "Tell me what's wrong with him. His voice sounds too frail."

Mierta turned his attention to Orlynd. He leaned forward and listened carefully for about a minute. "He's going on about something," Mierta responded, tilting his head, trying to understand Orlynd's words. "It is a series of words. He is repeating them, but I can't quite make them all out."

All three approached Orlynd, who was still lying on his back. His eyes were closed, and his head occasionally shifted as if he was suffering from a nightmare. His chest was rising and falling at a quickened pace.

Mortain lifted Orlynd's left hand and felt for a pulse, finding it strong and steady. He then checked his temperature, discovering his fever had lowered significantly. He gazed at Mierta with a look of bewilderment.

"Has his fever returned? Mortain, I demand an explanation for this madness he is uttering," Déor said.

Before Mortain could answer, Mierta leaned in and listened to Orlynd whispering.

"Well?" Déor asked a bit impatiently.

Mierta looked up and hesitated before suggesting, "I dare say it sounds like a poem."

"Yes? And what is he saying specifically?" Déor inquired, a bit too aggressively.

Mierta nodded his head nervously. He listened to the words again, then started repeating them. "When dual warlocks of royal blood reflect their image. A time of great peril will commence..."

Frustrated, Déor rubbed his hands through his hair.

"When dual warlocks of royal blood reflect their image?" he interrupted. "What utter nonsense could Orlynd be speaking of? There are no warlocks in the royal family. Could he be having some sort of fit because of his treatment? Or, perhaps fallen into madness?"

Déor said to himself. He glared over to Mierta. "Is that all he said? Again! Repeat."

"Yes, sire," Mierta answered. He stared down intently at the warlock, waiting for Orlynd to start muttering the words again when Orlynd's eyes abruptly opened and the warlock sat up.

Startled, Mierta jumped back.

"Orlynd?" Déor asked.

Promptly, Mierta walked to the edge of the bed and looked into Orlynd's face. He observed Orlynd was staring forward, his gaze appearing to look far away.

Mierta studied him for a good minute, noticing a remnant of flames displaying themselves in Orlynd's pupils. "Something is not right. I can see fire in his eyes."

"What?" Déor interrupted, suddenly recalling his father speaking of Orlynd having the ability to make predictions when his eyes appeared to have fragments of flames. "Record whatever he is uttering right now!"

Orlynd spoke again, this time with a voice that didn't sound like his own.

"When dual warlocks ay royal blood reflect their image, a time ay great peril will commence. Oan who is coerced will seek the betrayal ay power. The energy ay magic will serve the bearer who brings peace."

Orlynd stopped speaking, closed his eyes, and collapsed back against the pillow.

Déor quickly moved toward the bed, his eyes wide with shock. "Orlynd!" he cried. He could feel his pulse throbbing in his ears. He quickly turned his attention back to his court physician. "Mortain, please," Déor stammered, finding his voice. "Is he dying?" His eyes filled with tears, fearing the worst.

Again, Mortain checked Orlynd's pulse and temperature. "Sire, I do not understand how, but the fever has turned. He is sleeping naturally."

"Oh, thank the good Lord!" Déor responded. "When he wakes I must seek his counsel and apologise for doubting him. I shall be forever in his debt. He is a soothsayer, as my father said." He stood and walked towards the doorway of his private apartment.

"Your Grace, may I ask where you are going so urgently?"

"To locate my scribe. I need to make a proclamation clearing the O'Brien name. Send for me when Orlynd is conscious."

CHAPTER TWENTY-TWO

COINNEACH CASTLE
THE KINGDOM OF VANDOLAY
1238 CE

Orlynd, please accept my apologies," Déor began, approaching the bed. "I know you have just woken, but I must inquire about something you said earlier with urgency."

"Yir Grace?" Orlynd asked, confused, sitting up.

"Earlier, you said, 'When dual warlocks of royal blood reflect their image, a time of great peril will commence. One who is coerced will seek the betrayal of power. The energy of magic will serve the bearer who brings peace.' Please, I beseech you, what does this all mean?"

Orlynd looked at Déor, twisting his features. "Ah apologise, Yir Grace. Ah'm afraid Ah dinnae recall whit yis speak ay, though Ah recall ma father said Ah spoke thit once before."

Déor blinked, disbelief in his face. "Yes. My father said your eyes would…" Déor paused and ran his hand though his hair. "Forgive me. I cannot think of any other way to describe them other than looking like flames. I doubted your legitimacy, and for that I apologise with the utmost sincerity to both you and my father. I have disgraced his memory. However, I do question your prediction. You spoke of warlocks with royal blood. There has never been a warlock in the royal family. May this perhaps have been instead a warning that Aracelly means to invade my kingdom to end my reign? Certainly, you must know."

Orlynd frowned. "Ah dinnae know, Yir Grace. Lord told me nothing about an invasion."

"I see," Déor answered, disappointed. Perhaps Orlynd had spoken something he should not, and now was lying to cover his tracks. After the way he had treated the warlock, he could not blame him if he hated him. "I understand if you do not wish to clarify. I have given you no reason to believe you have earned my love. I admit I have wronged you. I was a terrible prince and I have not been a good king. This will change. I promise you and everyone else in this room, to be a good king, as my father was before me. God spared your life so that I may be able to fulfil this vow. I realise I will not be able to do this alone. I require my conscience by my side, but most important of all, I need the one that shall forever from this day forward be called my friend. Please, Orlynd, forgive me."

Mortain and Mierta exchanged uncomfortable looks at their king's words.

"Ah forgive yis, Yir Grace."

Déor decided to press a bit more. "Tell me, Orlynd, what is the last thing you remember?"

"The last thing Ah remember," Orlynd said, struggling to recall, "Ah looked intae the goblet n Ah realised at thit moment whit Ah had foreseen in ma Rite ay Wands wid never come tae be. Ah wid nae be thir tae save ma King." Orlynd looked into Déor's stunned face.

"Save me? Save me how? Please, explain," Déor urged.

"He can't," Mierta stated, interrupting, crossing his arms.

"Nonsense! Of course, he can. I am the King," Déor retorted.

"Mierta is right, Your Grace," Mortain answered. "Discussion of the Rite of Wands isn't permitted. Lord forbids it."

"Then, your Lord will make an exception. If my life is in danger, I should know about it!"

"With due respect, Your Grace, you already do. Someone deliberately poisoned your goblet. If Your Highness had drunk from the goblet instead, your life might have been forfeit. Therefore, Orlynd's wish to save you has already been fulfilled. You can ask no more of him."

"Yes, I suppose you are right. He has already proven his loyalty and therefore shall be appropriately rewarded," Déor stated. He reached into his tunic and pulled out a freshly inked scroll. "I, Déor, King of Vandolay, hereby decree the O'Brien name shall be cleared of all wrong-doing, and hence forth be forever welcome in my court."

Orlynd was deeply touched by the king's kindness; however, his mind was not at ease.

Déor noticed Orlynd's troubled expression. "I'm afraid that doesn't mean your father can return since it was my father who exiled him."

"Ah understand, Yir Grace, n Ah thank yis fir yir gesture. However, thit is nae whit troubles me," Orlynd replied. He could feel an imminent darkness lingering over the kingdom, and if his Rite of Wands had been accurate, war was still to come.

"What is it? If there is something else I may be able to do, say the word," Déor said.

Orlynd half-smiled at Déor. "Ah suppose it wid be tae much tae ask fir an upgrade in living facilities?" he joked.

PART TWO

CHAPTER TWENTY-THREE

TARLOCH CASTLE
GLENDALOW
1260 CE

Help him." Friedrich, a young man no older than his late twenties sniffed and peered up at Orlynd. Friedrich was sitting on a grey stone floor, which was stained with blood. They were in an old torture chamber located on the bottom level of the dungeons of Tarloch Castle. He was cradling his unconscious identical twin brother.

Whit has happened here? How did we git here n how can Ah help them? Ah cannae perform healing magic. Whit am Ah supposed tae do? Orlynd's mind raced.

The young man lying on the floor was nearly dead. Froebel, as he was called, was naked. Both of his shoulders had been dislocated. Additionally, a large wound, which began at his left shoulder blade, travelled down his back. It was swollen, covered in pus, and accompanied by reddened skin. His chest was covered with whip wounds.

His fevered face was ghostly pale, and his dark brown bangs clung in ringlets to his sweat-covered forehead. His bluish lips were open, and his breathing was rapid and laboured.

Orlynd's thoughts became distracted when he heard Friedrich cry, "My healing spell isn't working! He's getting worse." Orlynd observed that the young man was of royal descent, dressed in courtly attire. The crest of the Kingdom of Vandolay was on the front of his tunic and a manifested quartz crystal hung from a black string around his neck.

Orlynd's eyes fixated on the gem. It contained two crystals bonded as one and was wrapped in a golden wire. But that wasn't what caught Orlynd's attention. It was the distinct appearance of the two crystals pulsating with a white light. The smaller of the two was slowly growing dimmer. He had never seen anything like that before. It was an even bigger surprise to see the young man grasping in his right hand a wand crafted of Ziricote wood with a blue obsidian quartz crystal fused at the top.

A wand. Tis cannae be, Orlynd thought. *There has never been a warlock in the royal family!*

"Orlynd?" Friedrich asked with a tone of confusion. "Please, you must help him."

Friedrich's face grew ghostly pale just like his twin's. "Orlynd, please! Save him."

✕ ✕ ✕

ORLYND GASPED, abruptly opening his eyes. His breathing was rapid, his heart was racing, and his body was moist from sweat. Had it been just a dream?

Orlynd calmed himself. His room looked the same as it had the night before. This hadn't been the first time he had dreamt such a dream. What was this dream telling him? Was it a vision? A warning? What did it mean? Ever since he was a teenager he had been blessed, or cursed as he sometimes looked at it, with the gift of foresight. He never knew when, where, or how he would receive a vision, nor could he ever be certain if the vision would prove to be true.

He often pondered how his mother interpreted her dreams. Did she also have intense dreams? Did they ever mislead her, or were they always correct? What did she do with the information they provided? Had she let events come to pass, or had she intervened? Had she even foreseen her own death? These were questions Orlynd would never know the answer to.

His thoughts became distracted by a sudden loud knock coming from his front door.

Orlynd sighed and gathered a dressing gown from his bedroom closet. As he wrapped it around himself, he glanced in a small mirror. The years had been kind to him, all that showed was the beginnings of a scruffy beard. He tied the belt of his robe around his waist and made his way towards the front door.

MCKINNON ESTATE
GLENDALOW
1260 CE

"WELCOME HOME, Father," Lochlann announced, opening the door to the McKinnon Estate.

When the elder McKinnon entered, he noticed a cosy fire burning in the fireplace in the far corner of the main room. Straight ahead was a doorway, which led to the kitchen. And off to the left was the stairway leading to the sleeping quarters.

"My boys! It is good to be home," Mortain replied hugging Lochlann.

Mierta stood a bit back, studying his father's complexion as he rubbed his own prominent chin. Mortain's face displayed signs of exhaustion. His eyes were bloodshot and there were bags underneath them. His skin had a pasty white look and there was a glow from the beginnings of fever.

"I reckon you're both well?" Mortain smiled at Mierta.

"Yes, Father," Mierta answered, approaching. Perhaps the return trip had not been pleasant, or perhaps he had become ill. He promptly investigated further.

Mierta wrapped his arms around his father. He observed the distinction in his body temperature. Mierta wished to mask his worry, so he decided to distract himself with some light conversation. He placed his arm around his father and led the way. "Come into the parlour and have some tea. Armand had just made a fresh pot." He turned his head and raised his voice. "Armand, the tea!"

Mortain's eyes fell upon the cherrywood table and three matching comfy chairs and cups. Armand brought over a fresh pot of tea and set it in the middle of the table.

"Was your trip to Norhamptone successful? You must tell us all about it," Mierta grinned, taking a seat.

"Blimey! It is a bit chilly in here," Mortain said, taking a seat. He took a sip of the tea. "Mmm. Yes, I saw an old mate of mine," Mortain began. There was a hint of sadness in his voice. He took another sip. "Tiberius is exactly how I remember him, only, perhaps a bit frailer." There was worry in his eyes, perhaps even regret? He drank his tea until the cup was empty. "Forgive me, I've done too much. My body is not meant for such trips anymore." He stood up.

Mierta stood and quickly placed his arm around his father to support him.

"Thank you, my boy, but I can manage," Mortain answered. For a brief moment, their eyes met. Mierta glanced over to Lochlann. When he looked back, Mortain shot him a warning look.

"I will have Armand bring the tea to your room. You go and rest now," Mierta said in order to end the potential odd moment of silence. He watched his father leave the parlour and proceed towards the stairs. His smile turned to a frown, with his lips protruding in an expression of displeasure as he sat back down. He continued to drink his tea in silence, staring at the wall.

Lochlann chuckled, oblivious. "Mierta, I would almost charge you with not being happy our father is home."

Not amused, Mierta replied, "You cannot possibly have any idea." He sipped his tea and set it back down on the table.

"What is that supposed to mean?"

"Please tell me you are not so daft to have not noticed?" Mierta's eyes widened when he realised Lochlann really hadn't noticed. "Blimey, Lochlann, I swear it amazes sometimes that you are even my brother. I'm utterly gobsmacked. I must say, Mum and Dad certainly forgot to pass on to you their intelligence, and where on earth did you get that black hair?"

"I'm afraid I do not know what you are going on about, Mierta, but I think we should be celebrating the fact our father is home," Lochlann responded, standing. He walked towards the kitchen to rinse his finished cup of tea.

Mierta sighed. "Honestly, you're such a blubbering buffoon." He finished his tea, set the empty cup onto the table and headed towards the cellar.

The Rite of Wands had warned him of a plague that would ravage the lands of Iverna. Was it possible his father was ill with the very plague destined to kill him?

As soon as Mierta had reached the bottom of the stone staircase, he walked over to the middle of three workbenches, slamming his fists into the surface, tears forming in his eyes.

"Argh!" he yelled, sweeping the detritus of his last attempt at a cure off the workbench and onto the floor. The scalpel, pestle and mortar, and an empty gothic-styled silver candlestick, fell to the ground and shattered a large culture tube.

Why? Twenty-four years! Twenty-four years and I still haven't been able to conjure a cure!

He wiped his hands through his hair and breathed in and out slowly in order to calm himself.

Father cannot go to Poveglia. The disease will just continue to spread. If I cannot find a cure, I must discover a way to slow it down. The answer has got to be down here. I just have to find it.

He stared intensely at the bookshelf, containing a large, musty-smelling old book from his father's former medical collection. The book contained hundreds of pages of different potions, but Mierta was searching for one potion in particular, certain it contained the healing remedies for his ailing father.

Practically leaping across the room, he grabbed the book off the shelf. It was a bit heavier than he remembered, but he brought it back over to the table and dropped it. It landed with a large thud as dust flew everywhere. He had flipped through several pages before he became distracted by a loud knock coming from the front door.

"Bloody hell! Armand, will you get the door, please?" Mierta called from the cellar.

His father called him a genius, a mad genius sometimes, but he was determined to come up with a solution, even if that meant sacrificing captured animals. His intelligence was about to be put to the test, and he felt if he could not come up with a solution and his father was unable to make the journey to the Kingdom of Aracelly, hope would be lost.

He placed his finger alongside the text on the page while he intensely studied the ingredients, reading them aloud.

"Parsley, belladonna, toadstools, live salt water slugs," he said, getting lost in thought momentarily. "East Indians used slugs to numb gums, but it often led to parasites, which crawled from your stomach to your brain and tended to be toxic." He looked disgusted. "No. Won't do, absolutely won't do."

He flipped to another page and then another, again placing his finger alongside the text.

"Sodium bicarbonate, vinegar, peroxide, nightshade," he read, pausing for a brief moment, perplexed.

Abruptly, he shut the book and dropped it on the workbench.

"Well, that book is rubbish," he said, brushing his hands through his brown hair, making sections of it settle awkwardly.

As he rubbed his right hand over his large chin, he remembered he had put a ludicrous spell on the book so that anyone who tried to read it would not be able to understand in order to preserve his well-kept secret recipes. It was the same spell that had befuddled him as a child.

"Right," said Mierta, revealing his wand from his pocket and pointed it at the book. *"Arduescha ridícula!"*

His eyes twinkling, he watched the words become understandable again. He raised his wand again. "All right. Show me the recipe. *Mostravit!"*

He grinned with excitement as the book did as he commanded. It opened to a page three-quarters of the way through. His eyes danced while he quickly glanced at the page. He placed his wand back into his pocket. "Ha! This is it! Balsam, ammonium carbonate, camphor, glycerine, pine needle oil, and methanol. Blimey!"

He pranced around the cellar until he came to a wall, which was lined with shelves holding various books and equipment. First, he grabbed a cauldron, filled it with water, and set it to boil. Just as soon as he had gathered the ingredients, there was another set of knocks sounding from the door upstairs.

"Armand, the door!" Mierta shouted a bit louder, becoming annoyed by the continued distraction.

Opening the bottle of camphor, he sniffed, and immediately regretted the action as the piny aroma burned in his nostrils. He had just poured a small amount into the cauldron, when he heard the knocking again. Muttering to himself and wondering where his father's servant was, he turned back to the cabinet, accidentally picking up castor oil instead of pine needle oil.

"Armand!" Mierta looked in both directions and heard no sounds of footsteps. "Oh, do not bother. I will do it myself," he said to air. He placed the castor oil into the cauldron and walked up a set of stone stairs.

"Good evening, may I help you?" Mierta inquired after he opened the door. He watched the woman wearing a dark, simple cloak turn herself around and lower her hood.

"Your Majesty!" Mierta stated, a goofy grin hiding his surprise.

"Mierta," Queen Anya sneered, watching him bow and lower his face to kiss the top of her hand. "Let me pass. I have urgent business with my court physician."

CHAPTER TWENTY-FOUR

MCKINNON ESTATE
GLENDALOW
1260 CE

He's not here." Mierta frowned. Without a response, he watched Anya push past him and step inside. Mierta sighed and followed her.

"Where is he? Taking care of a patient I presume?" Anya said, looking about the room.

"Gone," Mierta said, closing the door behind them. "I don't know where. I don't keep track of him." Mierta lied. He normally would not be this cross with Anya, but his potion needed watching. "Is the interrogation over now? May I return to my business or is there something else you need, Your Majesty?"

Anya frowned slightly and cleared her throat. "My, when did we come to such inauspicious terms?" she uttered.

Mierta stared at the queen, his eyes telling her that he was not in the mood for any of her shenanigans. However, his thoughts drifted back to when he had first met Anya.

COINNEACH CASTLE
THE KINGDOM OF VANDOLAY
1228 CE

MIERTA OPENED the door and stepped out of the private apartment into the hall. He wanted to scream from excitement. Things may have not gone exactly to plan, however, he believed in his heart Ezekiel would be able to teach him everything he needed.

He became so lost in his own thoughts, it did not register the queen had been approaching from down the hall. He walked right into her.

Mierta glanced forwards, his eyes widening, realising he had carelessly bumped into the queen. "Your Grace," Mierta said, abruptly lowering himself to the ground. "Forgive me for my clumsiness."

Anya smirked and reached out her hand for Mierta to kiss. "Mierta is your name, is it not?"

"Yes, my name is Mierta," he spoke nervously.

"I understand you were one of the members who helped spare the life of our young soothsayer. Déor and I are most grateful for everyone's benevolence. Rise. Please, speak freely."

"You are more than kind," Mierta said. "I really did not have anything to do with it."

"Nonsense. There is no need to be modest. My little birds tell me you have talents, many, which have not been fully developed yet." She quickly looked him over, her eyes stopping at his crotch, feeling certain she could manipulate him just like she had other boys, even if he was a warlock. She brushed her finger against the bottom of his chin.

Mierta felt blood rise to his cheeks and his heart started to race. He glanced into the queen's eyes, afraid to further embarrass himself. "Thank you for your confidence, Your Grace," he replied nervously, looking away.

Anya laughed. "Please, there is no need to address me so formally. You may address me informally. From this day forward, you shall be permitted to address me as Anya. I expect I shall see more of you in court?"

"I reckon so, though it may be some time, Your Grace, I mean Anya," Mierta answered.

"And why, may I inquire, is that?" the queen answered. She was confident she was leaving a favourable impression on the warlock, observing Mierta's flushed cheeks and uneven breathing.

"I have been awarded an apprenticeship with the Apothecarist, Ezekiel Kavanagh. He is the one you should really be thanking for saving your soothsayer."

"Is that so?" Anya said, raising an eyebrow, intrigued. "Well, then, I expect to see great things from you in the future, Mierta."

MCKINNON ESTATE
GLENDALOW
1260 CE

"ALL RIGHT, I confess!" Anya said, bringing Mierta back to the present. "I lied. I didn't come here for business with my court physician. I came here to see you. I could not send a messenger and request an audience with you at the castle. It would be too risky. People would wonder."

"Wonder what?" Mierta asked, softening a bit from a small moment of sheer curiosity, but he still held his sour look. "What are you up to?"

"I rather dislike confrontation in an entry-way, but I have a proposal. I need a favour. Believe me," she said, walking towards him, using her body to get his attention, "you will be greatly reward-ed." She spoke in a flirtatious tone as she traced a finger down the left side of his cheek and then lightly blew in his ear, sending shivers down his spine.

"You got my attention," Mierta replied, eyeing her with a look of disgust. "There is no need for you to seduce me. Certainly, I have learned all of your tricks by now. You should be doing that with Déor. Tell me, has he stopped going to your bedroom again, ignoring his royal duty of a husband, because he realised what kind of wench you really are?"

Anya's eyes grew wide and she slapped him hard on the side of the face.

Mierta turned his face away, unbeknownst to Anya, smirking.

"How dare you speak of such things to me? I am your Queen!" She paused, becoming angrier by the minute. She could hear him snickering. "What is this mockery? Speak!"

He turned his face back to her, his eyes fuming. "I do not answer to the Kingdom of Vandolay. The only person I report to is *me!*"

"Preposterous. You may now live in Glendalow, but you still are a warlock; therefore, you owe your allegiance to Lord Kaeto, unless he has passed and Aracelly has no leader?"

"No, no, nothing like that," Mierta said, shaking away her notion. He continued, "But if you think for a moment I'm going to assist you in your plans, you are wrong," he sneered.

Then it occurred to him that he had completely forgotten about his potion. He responded by increasing the speed of speech and turned to walk away. "Now, I have other matters to attend to. If you'll excuse me…"

Anya forcefully grabbed both of his hands and coerced him to face her. She placed his hands directly over the bare skin above her breasts. "Mierta."

Mierta could feel her heartbeat under his hands, but he forced himself with every last inch of his mind to resist her advances. He thought she was attractive, and yet he was completely aware that she frequently enticed men. She was trying to entrap him, but she would fail. He was more cunning than she was. He was already onto her.

"Oh, stop it. I know what you are planning," he quieted his voice, leaning into the Anya's body and speaking into her ear. "It isn't going to work. I'm a very busy man. You don't want me to cast a spell on you."

They were both so much alike and the queen didn't even know it, which was a shame, really, because together, Mierta acknowledged to himself, *there would be nothing they couldn't accomplish.*

Defeated, Anya loosened her grip on his hands. "All right. You don't have to look so peevish. I can see you are going to be a challenge for me," she said, as she watched Mierta adjust his clothing. Her first impulse was to issue an order, but she thought better of it. Threatening him further would be a waste. It was obvious she could not control him. "I request you take me to where you make your potions, please. Prove to me that what I have heard of your genius was more than simple rumours."

"As you wish," he sulked, looking towards the ceiling. He gestured towards the cellar.

Anya responded by gesturing back, instructing him to take the lead.

Mierta sighed. He walked past Anya and started down the stairs. "Be careful of the rats," said Mierta, pausing, realising how incredibly awkward the next part would sound. "They like to hang around the stairs. Don't step on them, I've come to enjoy their company."

Anya half laughed. "Enjoy the company of rats? I would have never thought of such a preposterous suggestion."

ORLYND'S COTTAGE
THE KINGDOM OF ARACELLY
1260 CE

"HELLO?" ORLYND said, peeking out the door. When he felt a small tug on his dressing gown, he glanced downward. "Oh, hello, wee lad." Orlynd smiled, lowering himself to the boy's height. The boy had to be no older than six or seven. "Whit is yir name?"

"My name is Arthur, sir," the boy answered with a half-smile.

By the way the boy was dressed, Orlynd concluded Arthur was not from the Kingdom of Aracelly. He wore a second hand white cotton shirt, a pair of black breeches, which had a large rip in the left knee, an overcoat missing some buttons, and shoes falling apart at the heels.

"Arthur," Orlynd spoke, trying to figure out why the boy looked slightly familiar to him. He was certain Arthur couldn't be one of the royal family's trusted messengers, but then, why was he here? Was he perhaps lost? "Tell me, where ur yir mam n dad? Ur yis lost?"

"No, sir," Arthur responded, "my parents are home."

"N where is hame? Huv yis travelled far?" Orlynd questioned, becoming more befuddled.

"Yes, sir," Arthur replied. "From the Kingdom of Vandolay, sir. My older brother was supposed to deliver this to you, but he's real sick with a rash, a fever, and a sore throat. Here you are, sir." The boy pulled a white envelope that had been folded in half from his overcoat.

Orlynd watched intently as Arthur handed him the note. "Thank yis, Arthur."

Orlynd flipped over the letter, discovering it contained a great blue seal of the realm indicating it was something important about a member of the royal family of Vandolay.

Orlynd sighed deeply. Then he realised why Arthur looked familiar to him. He furrowed his forehead in worry.

"Arthur," Orlynd said, placing the letter safely into his bathrobe pocket for safekeeping for later. His worried eyes gazed at the boy. "Yis said yir older brother wis sick? Is yir older brother named Seamus?"

Arthur nodded.

"Huv yis fetched the court physician?" Orlynd asked with concern in his voice.

"No, sir. The court physician could not come out to our house. He is not seeing people anymore. Mum was crying and said he is really sick, too. She thinks he may be dying."

"Blimey," uttered Orlynd. Multiple thoughts flew through his mind. Seamus had most likely not been seen by anyone else, which made the situation even more perilous. Judging from the state of Arthur's shoddy attire, his family most likely could not afford the trip to the Kingdom of Aracelly to have Seamus seen by the healers at the sanatorium.

"Tell yis whit, Arthur," Orlynd replied. "Ah'm going tae help yis git Seamus well again. Jist give me a moment, stay right thir." Orlynd stood up and went back into the house to fetch some money. After a minute of searching through a dresser in his bedroom where he kept extra cash around in case of an emergency, he returned back to Arthur. He lowered himself down again to Arthur's height. "Give me yis hand."

Arthur did as Orlynd told him.

Orlynd placed the money in the palm of his hand. "Tell ye mam nae tae worry. She can git Seamus tae the kingdom ay Aracelly n thir is enough tae buy all ay yis new clothes. Oan yis go."

"Thank you, sir. Bless you!" Arthur exclaimed.

Orlynd smiled. He watched Arthur run down the dirt pathway towards the centre of the kingdom. Once he was out of sight, Orlynd went back into his cottage. He sat down on his bed and opened the letter.

Inside was a summoning, a request for Orlynd's presence at Coinneach Castle to have an audience with the King of Vandolay pertaining to important matters regarding his upcoming coronation celebration.

CHAPTER TWENTY-FIVE

MCKINNON ESTATE
GLENDALOW
1260 CE

No! No! No! No!" Mierta exclaimed, smelling something burning. He raced down the stairs to discover the cauldron containing his potion, its contents boiling over onto the table. "Ouch!" he yelped, burning the fingertips of his right hand. Unsuccessfully trying to remove the potion from the flames, he set the cauldron down on the table in front of him.

"What in God's name?" Anya responded, watching him quickly blow into the pot, trying to cool its contents. "I can assure you, Mierta, you won't succeed in cooling it down doing that."

"Would you please silence your tongue for just a moment, so I can hear myself think!" Mierta snapped. "I told you I was engaged." He muttered something to himself, which was incomprehensible to Anya, before bolting over to the cabinet in order to find something that could help salvage his masterpiece.

"Mierta, calm yourself. You have yet to hear my proposal."

"I do not desire to know what it is," Mierta answered, making all kinds of noise while searching various tables before squatting in front of the cabinet.

"I see. So, this is where you keep all of your potions?" the queen inquired, changing the subject. She raised an eyebrow as she watched Mierta frantically search through the cabinet, occasionally knocking over a bottle of ingredients. She knew what she came for had to be in the cellar, but she didn't know exactly where.

"Yes? Were you expecting them to be somewhere else?" he asked with a tone of annoyance.

"Mierta, would you stop being so cross! I am merely admiring your work," she replied, trying to discover the location of a particular potion. Perhaps she would not even need to ask for Mierta's assistance.

"Correct me if I'm wrong, but you're only interested in my business when you want something." Mierta's eyes brightened and a huge grin appeared on his face when he discovered a single stirrer located towards the back of the cabinet.

"That's absolutely ludicrous," Anya said.

"Is it?" Mierta challenged, grabbing the stirrer and walking back to the cauldron on the table. He rapidly stirred the potion.

"Mierta?" Anya stated, watching him. "Mierta, are you even listening to me? I need your help."

He raised a hand up to silence Anya.

Shock displayed over her face and he lowered his hand. Anger was quickly building inside her. How dare he tell her to be quiet!

About a minute later, he placed the stirrer down, and carefully dipped his finger into the concoction. He placed the tip of his finger into his mouth, tasting a small sample of the mixture.

"Still not cold enough," Mierta spoke to himself, dissatisfied, finishing licking the contents off his finger. He thought he could detect something off about the concoction, but he decided to ignore it. Instead, he reached into his breeches' pocket for his wand.

"What on earth are you doing, now?" Anya pondered.

"I'm being clever, or you could call it cheating. It's still too hot," Mierta said, raising his wand just above the opening of the cauldron. "I have to get the temperature just right." He made a clockwise motion with his wand and commanded, *"Tiofria!"*

A large amount of cloudy white mist rose from inside the cauldron as the contents cooled to just below room temperature.

Anya stared, uncertain of how to respond. Mierta was one of the most talented warlocks she had ever been associated with and rarely had she seen him so distracted. She sensed an urgency that was completely unlike him.

"Mierta," she began, carefully taking his hand into hers as she watched him continue to stare at the cauldron. "What's wrong, and don't you dare lie to me and say it is nothing. Speak. I am your Queen and your friend. Allow me to help you."

"You can't," Mierta frowned, shaking her hand away. "Whatever you are plotting in that little head of yours isn't going to happen. I'm not interested in any help you can give." He paused as his emotions were starting to become too much. His voice quivered as he revealed, "My father has Shreya." He turned to Anya when he heard her gasp.

She covered her mouth with her hands.

Worry displayed across his face as he continued. "I reckon he became exposed when he recently journeyed to Edesia to visit an old mate." Then he lowered his glance, his face hardening. He turned his face away and started concentrating back on his potion. "Lochlann doesn't know yet, so don't inform him. He doesn't need to know, not yet."

Anya lowered her hands and uttered, "Your father has the plague? I have been exposed!"

"Nonsense," Mierta answered. "You haven't been exposed long enough to be infected. Only my father and I have."

She looked sternly at Mierta. "How dare you be so careless and allow me to enter your home during such circumstances! I slapped you, I touched you. It is my royal duty to protect my kingdom from illness. I am their rock, their leader. This entire estate should be quarantined immediately! You have permitted death to penetrate the lands of Iverna."

"*No!*" Mierta yelled, slamming his hand against the table, startling Anya. His body trembled, and tears started to form in his eyes. He told himself he would not display his emotions, and he would not show weakness, especially to Anya. "I can reverse the disease." He blinked the tears back, took a deep breath and calmed himself. "Before you showed up I was constructing a potion to slow down the symptoms."

"How?"

"With this!" Mierta exclaimed, raising his hands out in front of him as he displayed his masterpiece. "It's a mixture meant to lower fevers and stop the most enduring coughs. Comes from a formula I created during my apprenticeship." He reached for a small culture tube on the table and poured some of the liquid from the cauldron into it.

Mierta eyed it carefully, hoping this mixture would work, then tilted his head back and raised the culture tube to his lips.

Anya interrupted before he was able to consume any of the contents, "And if it should fail?"

Mierta gazed at Anya, annoyed. "I don't know yet. I haven't thought that far into the future. I'll come up with something else." He wasted no further before ingesting the mixture.

However, before he was able to swallow, his face displayed distress. His hand grasping the small culture tube abruptly opened, sending the culture tube straight to the floor. Glass shattered at his feet.

"Mierta?"

As the flavours materialised inside his mouth, his brain detected something very wrong. It was the most disgusting-tasting potion he had ever created. He could not even imagine someone being tortured could endure it.

Anya became very concerned at the sound of his gagging. "Mierta, what's happening? What's wrong?"

Mierta raised his hands to his mouth, desperate to not further embarrass himself in front of Anya. His body shuttered and jerked awkwardly as he rushed to find an empty cauldron.

"What is this madness? Are you having some sort of fit?" Anya asked.

Mierta raced to the cabinet and found one just in time. He leaned over, gasping after spitting out the contents of the mixture. "Castor oil."

"Castor oil?" Anya said.

Mierta lifted his head as he instantly recognised what was wrong with the concoction. "Yes, castor oil. Castor oil is known for its particular odour and taste." He leaned again into the cabinet to investigate, pulling out a small bottle containing a very light yellow liquid. "Aha! As suspected, it was substituted for needle oil. There was nothing wrong with my potion. It shall just have to be to be remade."

While Anya watched Mierta gather the ingredients necessary to prepare the concoction, she had a fascinating idea. "I believe we can help each other. My father, the Hand of the King, is in need of a new potion maker at Tarloch Castle. I shall appoint you for the job in exchange for a favour. You will have full access to all areas of the castle, including the primary area in which you will be working, the dungeons."

"Well, dare I say it would be quite the challenge," Mierta smiled. Then he realised the dungeons of Tarloch Castle were filled with nothing but prisoners waiting for their deaths. Mierta's jaw dropped in disbelief. "There are criminals in those dungeons, people who have done terrible things! Why would I want to help criminals?"

Anya laughed. "My dear Mierta. Sometimes you can be very dense. You need subjects you can test your potions on willingly. Do not think of them as people. They gave up that title and right when they were arrested. What you decide to do with them is up to you."

Mierta crossed his arms. "So, you are going to offer me this position in exchange for what exactly? What kind of favour do you need from me?"

Anya lifted her face snobbishly. "I need to eliminate the king. The anniversary of his coronation is coming up in a few days, and I am confident I can execute the perfect plan to be rid of him with your assistance."

"You do realise that if your plan fails you will be tried for treason. We could both end up in the dungeons of Tarloch Castle or worse," Mierta warned. "I wouldn't want to witness the loss of that pretty little head of yours."

"My plan won't fail. It's too perfect not to."

"Then what is it?" Mierta asked impatiently.

"You," Anya replied, pointing a finger at him. "You are going to help me recreate a potion, and not just any potion, mind you, but one containing the same poison that killed his father. The original potion creator met an unfortunate end."

Mierta stared at Anya uneasily.

CHAPTER TWENTY-SIX

COINNEACH CASTLE
THE KINGDOM OF VANDOLAY
1260 CE

O rlynd walked down a long hallway that ran the length of Coinneach Castle. The walls were stained a dark red, and the flooring was made of cherrywood. As he walked down this hallway, he couldn't help but feel the eyes of the ancestors of the royal family were watching him. If it weren't for the many strategically placed windows, the hall would have been in complete darkness.

As Orlynd approached an intercepting hallway, he could hear footsteps coming toward him. And at the very instant he reached the interacting hall, the warlock Lochlann stepped out of the hallway and joined him.

Orlynd glanced to the side where the man was walking beside him. He stopped as his blood ran cold.

Lochlann continued to walk down the hallway when he noticed Orlynd had stopped and appeared to be staring at him. He slowed and turned around. "Um? Excuse me, is there something I can assist you with? May I dare suggest you look like you've just seen a ghost?"

At first Orlynd didn't say anything, for he was absorbed in his own thoughts. After a few moments he came to his senses and allowed his racing heart to calm. He breathed deeply and then laughed with embarrassment. "Sorry. Forgive me fir ma rudeness. Ah dinnae mean tae stare. Yis reminded me ay someone Ah used tae know. Ah wis oan ma ain tae huv an audience wi His Majesty. Yis must be new tae His Majesty's court? Ah huv nae seen yis around here before."

"I am sorry to disappoint, but I'm not a member of His Majesty's court," Lochlann answered, studying Orlynd curiously. "Your speech, is that Lorritish? You must be a diplomat from Edinbraugh, I presume?"

"Nae," Orlynd countered. "Ah wis born in the kingdom ay Aracelly. Ah reckon ma mam wis fi Edinbraugh in Lorrina. Ah'm a member ay the king's court."

"Oh. You're a warlock like myself then. Shame we have never met before. Perhaps we could share a fine drink at Brishen's next time you might be travelling to the Kingdom of Aracelly?" Lochlann smiled. "I don't suspect this will be the last time I see you. I live in Glendalow now, but I can never turn down a social invitation. Anyway, I'm here to have an audience, too, but with the queen. I am an old friend of hers, and, you're a member of the king's court? Who you are precisely?"

"Ma name is Orlynd. Ah am His Majesty's advisor. N yis?"

"An advisor, fancy that. My name is Lochlann," Lochlann responded. "Forgive me. The queen is expecting me, and I do not wish to delay her further. Perhaps I shall see you again, Or?"

"Orlynd," Orlynd corrected.

Lochlann nonchalantly smiled. "Mm. It was nice to meet you, Orlynd."

Orlynd stood still like a statue. He intently watched Lochlann turn and continue down the hallway towards the queen's private apartment. There was an extreme uneasiness in the pit of his stomach. The warlock looked exactly like Tiberius, minus the religious attire. He had the same dark, oily hair with the same piercing brown eyes. However, he was thin, and slightly shorter than Orlynd and maybe about ten years younger. The uncanny resemblance had to be a mere coincidence, for his father had been exiled nearly thirty years ago, and both his mother and younger brother had perished. Yet something about this man deeply troubled him. There was a fear in his heart he could not place.

It was like Lochlann had said. He had seen a ghost.

× × ×

"ARE YOU pleased, Your Majesty?" the Lady of the Bedchamber questioned, adding a five-strand pearl choker around the queen's neck.

Queen Anya sat in front of her vanity in Coinneach Castle located in the Kingdom of Vandolay. Singing to herself with an angelic soprano voice, she stared at her reflection proudly in the hand mirror. Her eyes intensely gazed as she observed her Lady of the Bedchamber manipulate her long, ginger-blonde hair into a beautiful braided bun. She finished by gently pinning a tiara into the top of Anya's bun.

Anya replied, "Do not ask such a foolish question, child. Do you wish me displeased?"

Vanessa kept her eyes averted to the floor and waited until the queen permitted her to speak.

"A thousand pardons, my lady," Vanessa said nervously, displaying her inexperience. "I will not ask such questions again. Please allow me to assist you into your dress."

"Granted."

Anya stood and looked off into the distance without giving further attention to her servant, as she was assisted into her purple and cream coloured gown for the evening.

A small smile crept to the corners of her mouth as she secretly imagined the results of the upcoming celebration of the king's coronation in three days. She expected the warlock Lochlann's arrival at any time. She had sent him a letter, urging him to seek an audience with her. She had schemed the most unprecedented plan starring Lochlann as a pawn in her giant chessboard.

Her thoughts were interrupted by a loud knock at the door. "What is it?"

"The warlock Lochlann to see you, Your Majesty," Aonghus nervously mumbled.

The page was also a new servant to Anya, a boy of no more than eleven. He guarded her bedroom from unwelcome guests, much to Queen Anya's annoyance.

"Let him come," she answered, raising an eyebrow, as Vanessa finished misting her with her favourite perfume.

Aonghus opened the door to let the warlock in.

"That will be all, thank you." Anya addressed Vanessa and waited until both of her servants had taken their leave.

× ✕ ×

"YIR MAJESTY," Orlynd said, bowing before the king, after he had been permitted to enter the king's private apartment for an audience.

"Orlynd." Déor smiled. "Thank you for coming. I seek your counsel today."

Orlynd lowered his gaze towards the ground and positioned his hands inside his brown robe as he rose. He waited for Déor to continue speaking.

Déor stood up from a chair in front of a table filled with wooden soldiers and ships, strategically set for battle. He walked towards a window that had been left slightly ajar. "The anniversary of my coronation is quickly approaching, and while my heart should be filled with joy, I find myself troubled."

The fifteenth of October was a day of commemoration, celebrating the anniversary of King Déor's coronation. It began in the morning with a traditional royal party hunt, which spread across the vast lands of the kingdom to the border of Glendalow and the Kingdom of Aracelly. Using the game the royal hunting party killed, Déor rewarded his subjects with a feast, acknowledging their loyalty.

"May Ah ask whit is troubling Yir Majesty?"

Déor stared outside the window and focused on his garden. "I received a letter containing grave news from Edesia. I have been informed their country has been hit by plague. Hundreds have already fallen ill, and many have perished. King Henrik has implemented a quarantine of the country immediately, and requests all carriages avoid the area until further notice. I worry the plague will spread here. Make haste, and share this information with the Kingdom of Aracelly."

"Aye, Yir Majesty," Orlynd answered. He waited for Déor to dismiss him. "Is thir something else, Yir Majesty?"

Déor hesitated. He glanced back at Orlynd for a brief moment before turning around. He took in a deep breath. "Yes. I realise it is not the time for personal matters, but my mind will not be at ease. I have been having this recurring dream involving a buck, doe, and their two fawns. The buck and the doe are killed, and a dragon carries the fawns away. I fear God has become displeased with me, and there is a coup manifesting behind my back in my court."

Orlynd could see the hidden pain in Déor's face. "May Ah ask yis, how yis came tae this conclusion?"

"My queen aggravates me," Déor explained as he paced. "She has been unable to bless me with an heir. It is making people question my ability to rule when there are none to reign after me." Déor stopped and stared directly at Orlynd. "We may be on good terms with Edesia now, but I assure you King Henrik would like nothing better than to overthrow me and claim Iverna as his own."

"Thit cannae happen, Yir Majesty," Orlynd stated.

"And what would bring you to such a conclusion?" Déor asked a bit irritated.

"Ah beg fir yis tae listen. The prophecy states thir shall be identical lads. Dinnae despair, Yir Majesty. Yir lineage shall continue! Yis shall huv children."

"And what does this derisible prophecy also state, Orlynd?" Déor interrupted. "How about that it will bring destruction to my kingdom? I will hear no more of it."

"Aye, Yir Majesty," said Orlynd, defeated. If only he could tell Déor about his reoccurring dream, but even then, it would not bring Déor comfort.

Déor calmed himself. "I shall visit Anya in her bedchambers tonight to demonstrate my continued love. May God bless our union and allow her to give me a child," Déor said. "There is one other matter I would like to discuss with you. At my coronation celebration, I wish for my guide to be at my side as a part of the royal party. It would be my honour to have you accompany me during the hunt. Do you accept?"

Orlynd raised his eyes and peered at Déor. "Ah shall dae as Yir Majesty wishes."

"It is settled then," Déor smiled. "You are permitted to leave."

Orlynd removed his hands from inside his brown robe and raised his hood over his face. He turned to leave and took a few steps forward. He then stopped, lost in his thoughts.

"What? What is it?" Déor inquired.

Orlynd hesitated, then turned back towards Déor and lowered his hood. He furrowed his eyebrows. "Yir Majesty, in court today Ah met a warlock who claimed tae be a friend ay Anya. He said his name wis Lochlann. If Ah may request, Ah need information oan the identification ay this man."

"Lochlann?" recalled Déor. "Yes, he is one of Mortain McKinnon's boys. Mierta is the older brother. You do not recall they helped save your life?"

"Aye, Yir Majesty. Ah huv nae forgotten their kindness," Orlynd answered.

Déor nodded, continuing. "The queen has a friendship with them not unlike our own. Lochlann is the least strange of the lot. They reside in Glendalow. Why? Has Lochlann done something I should be concerned about?" Déor questioned.

Orlynd smiled and held back a chuckle. "Nae, Yir Majesty," he answered with relief, concluding there was no resemblance between his father and the warlock. "Forgive me. Ma memory must huv momentarily failed me."

× ✕ ×

LOCHLANN APPROACHED Anya, genuflected and pressed his lips to her hand.

She turned her head away, barely able to hide her disdain. His oily, black hair fell over his face. She waited until he had stood back up and placed his hands inside his blood red and black robe with gold accents.

"Do you still love me?" Anya questioned.

"Yes, Your Majesty, I love you like the first day I set my eyes upon you. My love for you shall never change."

The corners of her mouth turned up slightly as she rose from her couch. She lightly traced her finger along the jawline of the warlock until she reached the tip of his chin, before gracefully moving away from him and setting her palm on the back of the couch. "Would you do anything for me?" she asked as she elegantly walked across the room and opened the drawer of her vanity.

He answered with surprise. "Why, Your Majesty, I would do anything you ask of me. Do you not know this?"

"Indeed," she replied. With her back to the warlock, she pulled out a small vial of liquid. She slipped the vial between the cleft of her breasts and clenched a pouch in her right hand. A small grin caressed the queen's lips as she swung around and let out a laugh. "I know this, my Lochlann. That is why I request you do this for me."

Lochlann knelt down in front of her. "I will do whatever Your Majesty requires of me."

Anya stared at Lochlann. Soon she would know his true allegiance. "You may rise," she said. Lochlann slowly stood up. He looked directly at Anya as she spoke again. "There is one more thing." With a seductive gleam in her eye, she removed the vial from her cleavage.

Lochlann immediately recognised the grey coloured vial. He watched as she twirled it around in her hand. He tried his best to hide his surprise.

"Forgive me," Lochlann said, after clearing his throat. "I did not know Your Majesty had interest in potions."

"Preposterous," Anya answered. She stood and held the vial out towards Lochlann. "Have a look if you wish." With a disdainful look, she handed the potion to Lochlann.

Lochlann opened the vial and inspected its contents. "There is only one warlock capable of concocting such a mixture. It must have been difficult to obtain it from Mierta willingly."

"Nonsense, Mierta was happy to oblige once I bestowed upon him the duty of my father's new potion maker. He'll be able to test all of his new potions on the prisoners to be executed!"

"That will be quite an improvement in his current situation. I'm sure he will be thrilled to test his potions on people instead of rats," Lochlann jested. "But, why did you request my presence?"

"Why, my dear, Lochlann," she said, approaching him. She traced her finger against the bottom of his chin once more before placing her hands gently around his cheeks. "I am confident you will see the plan through." She gracefully walked back to the couch. "The celebration of Déor's coronation approaches, and this year's celebration will not be forgotten."

"Are you ordering me to kill Déor? If this should fail I will lose my head!" Lochlann protested.

"And *that*, Lochlann," she spoke with a threatening gleam in her eyes, "is why you will succeed."

"Of course," Lochlann quickly answered, with a hint of uncertainty. "How would Your Highness suggest I proceed?"

Anya's cheeks flushed. She smiled with nervous anticipation. Soon the Kingdom of Vandolay would be hers. She just needed Lochlann to fulfil her wish.

"Déor presently has twice as many servants testing his food and drink," Anya stated. "It is appropriate for the occasion. He is beloved among our subjects. You will not be able to slip it into his meals without notice. Seek out Eoghan, leader of bandits. He owes me a favour. You will find him at his usual hangout—the back alleys.

"Instruct him to cover his arrows with the bottle's contents. He will know what to do. Tell him he will be greatly rewarded on the condition that he succeeds. The queen shall personally clear his name of any wrongdoing, including the charge of poaching of Déor's deer, and there will be no further discussion of the incident. You never saw him, nor did you ever speak to him. But if he should fail, or if he should mention anything that would be threatening, he will be executed."

CHAPTER TWENTY-SEVEN

MCKINNON ESTATE
GLENDALOW
1260 CE

M y son, is that you?" Mortain asked, catching sight of a shadow in the candlelight.

"Yes, Father," Mierta said.

"Come, sit beside me. I have to tell you something important," Mortain said, between coughs.

Mierta walked into the room, carrying a tray containing an empty bowl, a dry rag, a pot of cool water, and a cup of his latest attempt at a remedy. He set them down on the night table and sat down in the chair by the bed. "Shh. You must save your strength," he comforted.

"Mierta. I need to tell you something," Mortain whimpered.

"There will be plenty of time for you to tell me whatever it is, but right now you must rest."

"No. I must tell you now," he spoke, coughing several times again.

"All right," Mierta answered, a bit unnerved. He took a seat in the chair beside the bed. He reached and squeezed his father's hand, noticing the heat coming off him. "Tell me what you need to say."

"Lochlann. He's not…"

"Lochlann is fine," Mierta insisted. "He was summoned by the queen for an audience. I do reckon he will be given a royal title soon." He smirked, thinking about Lochlann's feelings for Anya. He stopped when he observed his father's shivering. Worry displayed across his face. Mierta loosened his grip and stood. He laid a cool hand over his father's brow. "Your fever is worse. The disease is progressing. I brought you something to slow it down." He reached over for the cup.

"Lochlann," Mortain started again, trying hard to get words out.

Mierta gazed at his father, confused.

"No, Father, it's me, Mierta. Lochlann will be home later."

The fever may be causing hallucinations.

"Here," Mierta said, carefully handing his father a cup filled with the brewed potion. He placed an arm behind his father's back and helped him up. "Drink it quickly. I reckon the flavour is repulsive."

Mortain obeyed. When he was finished, he immediately started coughing. He moaned when the fit eased.

"Chest hurts," he whimpered.

"I know. Roll onto your side," Mierta instructed. "Remember you taught me how to loosen congestion?" Mierta pounded on his father's back. He could feel his father's breathing begin to ease. Gently, he repositioned his father onto his back.

"Yes, my boy," he stated, his voice breathy. "You were very young, then. Hadn't had your eighth birthday yet. Your mum was proud."

"Yes. Yes, she was," Mierta answered, half-smiling. "Listen to me. Let's not talk about Mum right now. You need to save your strength."

"Tiberius is dead."

"Pardon?" Mierta questioned, baffled.

"I lost my best mate," Mortain said, tears starting to fall down his cheeks. "He sent me a letter. He thought I could help. I reckon he believed if he had informed me he already had the illness, I would have refused his offer. Many people in Edesia were sick. I treated those I could, but they all succumbed as I knew they would," Mortain disclosed.

"How?" Mierta asked, glancing over to him after pouring water into the bowl. He dipped the rag into it and rung it out. He gently brushed it against his father's brow.

"It was in my Rite of Wands," Mortain confessed.

Mierta stopped, taken aback by what his father had just revealed. Only witches and warlocks were allowed to participate in the Rite of Wands ceremony. His father was a man. There was no possible way he could have seen this grim future, unless…

No, Mierta denied. *It cannot be true. It's impossible. He cannot possibly know what he is going on about. My potion is clearly ineffective. His temperature must be getting worse.*

"Don't talk. Please, rest," Mierta stated with a sense of urgency, continuing to wipe the sweat from his father's face. Even if there was a tiny bit of truth behind what his father was saying, Mierta couldn't allow his father to discuss it. The Rite of Wands was supposed to be kept secret.

"You must understand, my son. I once desired to be an Apothecarist like you. I studied at Poveglia in the Kingdom of Aracelly. Only the brightest and most talented witches and warlocks are permitted to seek an apprenticeship there," Mortain explained.

Mierta's eyes grew wide. Things were beginning to make sense. He recalled when he was first welcomed into the magical community, his father had known about certain things that ordinary men wouldn't. Mierta always assumed he had gained this knowledge serving at court, or maybe even from when his mother was still alive. But, if his father had actually participated in the Rite of Wands ceremony himself, then, that could only mean one thing.

Mierta took a deep breath before continuing to inquire. He had to know even if whatever answer he would receive would pain him. "Father," Mierta said carefully, "are you trying to tell me you are a Magulia?"

Mortain did not respond.

"You are, aren't you?" Mierta asked, furrowing his forehead. "What happened?"

Again, Mortain did not answer.

"Father, forgive me, I must break a rule and tell you something that I should not. Those people—it was in my Rite of Wands, too. I know I am going to die if I cannot stop the disease. I am afraid. I do not want to fail. Tell me, please, what happened to you," Mierta confessed. When for a third time his father remained silent, Mierta lost his temper and shouted, "Tell me!"

Before Mortain could answer, another coughing fit overtook him and the feeling of something wet making contact with Mierta's skin interrupted his concentration. Mierta looked down to see a small, blood-tinged sputum lying on the top of his arm.

CARA FOREST
THE KINGDOM OF VANDOLAY
1260 CE

"YOUR MAJESTY, I strongly advise you to not go wandering off on your own!" Tierney had insisted after Déor unexpectedly announced he would be leaving the hunting party and heading into Cara Forest. He carried a white flag with the O'Connor family crest and a shield with a citrus tree in the middle. A knight's helmet surrounded by green lace was positioned directly above the shield.

"Nae," King Déor answered, brushing away a clump of his dark brown, curly hair. He jumped down from his horse. "I must locate the young lady who is crying. She may be injured."

"But, Your Majesty, no one is crying!" Aindrias maintained. He turned to Orlynd, who was accompanying them on horseback. He gestured with his hand. "Tell him, Orlynd."

Orlynd was distracted by what sounded like a high-pitched moaning coming from the western side of the forest. The longer he focused on the crying, it became clearer that it wasn't just crying, it was keening. Keening was a traditional form of vocal lament for the dead, often found in Iverna and Lorrina. The fact Déor could hear it too was most troubling, for the keening could be coming from a mythical spirit called the banshee. Only those families who were cursed could hear the banshee before either they were killed or someone close to them was killed.

"Orlynd?" questioned Tierney, Aindrias's son, who had followed his father into the guard. "You're a soothsayer. Did you hear anything? Anything at all? Orlynd?" Tierney waved his brown staff in Orlynd's direction as he spoke.

Orlynd took in a deep breath, blinked, and lowered the hood of his brown robe. He cleared his throat. "Nae wahn is crying Yir Majesty," he lied, looking directly into Déor's blue-grey eyes.

Suddenly one of the hounds found its prey's trail again and let out a loud set of barks. "Take my horse and continue following the hounds," Déor commanded. "I will meet with you both later."

"Déor," spoke Orlynd. "Be careful. Ah sense much misfortune."

Déor smiled as he unsheathed his ever trusty sword, Ruairí, and held it out near his side.

"Do not fear, my friend. I shall return safely soon."

THE CRACKLING of fallen leaves and the snapping of broken twigs could be heard underneath King Déor's feet as he wandered aimlessly through Cara Forest. The forest, which was normally full of bright red leaves for miles, was covered in a deep, misty fog. The hounds from the royal hunting party could be heard barking in the distance as they continued to search for their prey.

After a short time, Déor briefly saw the silhouette of a young woman in the fog but the figure quickly disappeared. "My lady, you should not be out here. It is not safe," he said, carefully stepping across a rivulet. "Please, let me know where you are so I can help you!"

As he continued west towards the source of the crying, the louder the sound became. Soon, a woman with long, silver hair appeared. She was dressed in a white gown that swirled in the grass around her feet, standing alone, with her back turned towards him.

Déor placed his sword back in its sheath. "Please, my lady," he said, reaching out a gentle hand.

The woman's crying immediately stopped, but her face was still turned away from him.

"Are you injured?" Déor inquired. "Do not be frightened."

She turned around and let out a shriek. Age had not been pleasant to her. Her face was deathly thin and decaying. The bones of her face protruded and there were patches of baldness on her head. Her eyes were bloodshot and demonic.

"Begone, you foul creature!" Déor cried, raising his sword and stepping back.

She shrieked again and approached him.

"Why are you here?" Déor recognised her to be the banshee from the stories he was told as a young prince. His family was haunted by an omen; a woman dressed in white. Whenever she appeared, it meant only one thing: *death*.

"Have you come to claim my life? Is that why you drew me out here? Speak, and trouble my family no more!"

She looked into the eyes of Déor. Slowly she brought her finger up to her lips and she spoke in a long drawn out whispery voice, *"Klaocala."*

She transformed and disintegrated into a thick, white glue-like substance as an arrow flew through what remained of her body. Déor gasped and stumbled a few steps back. He reached towards his right breast and grasped the arrow that had punctured his tunic.

He then saw Eoghan standing with his bow drawn.

"Y...y...you!" stated Déor between rapid breaths. "You shot me. Why?"

"You think you're such a great king? Your people in Deermid's Fields in Glendalow are starving! All of their potato crops are dying! They begged for a share of your grain, and what have you done? Ignored them!"

"Nay," Déor tried to reply. This terrible news about his people's crops was the first he had heard. Someone had deliberately kept this information from him.

Eoghan lowered his bow and walked up directly to Déor and pushed the arrow further into his body. "This is for the two men you killed. Long live the King!"

The sound of horses from the royal party coming their way echoed Déor's anguished cry.

Eoghan ran into the fog.

"Stop," King Déor cried as he collapsed.

Déor grasped the arrow that had punctured his chest. He took in a throbbing breath and pulled the arrow out. The pain was so intense, but the wail that escaped his lips brought him strength.

The arrow before him was covered in his blood and an unknown substance, which was rapidly changing the colour of his blood to something metallic.

What evil is this? Déor thought.

He took a painful breath, while a loud, high-pitched ringing filled his ears. Dark clouds began to form in his vision. He could feel his heart quickly beating as he attempted to stand. Holding out a hand to keep his bearings, he took one step and stumbled to the ground.

Still clutching the arrow with his left hand, he reached forward with his right and felt the ground beside him. His vision was gone. He paused and then stood again. Taking one more step forward, he faltered, and took several more steps sideways before finding the ground again. He rolled himself onto his back and lay against the red fallen leaves, hoping the feeling would pass. Refusing to allow himself to give in to the darkness, he reached up and grasped the gem hanging from a black string around his neck.

Slowly Déor closed his eyes, loosened the grip around the arrow, and began to give in to the poison. He felt in his heart his life was forfeit, but he hoped somehow the Bynoch would provide him the strength to continue on.

A pool of blood quickly formed next to him, and a strange, fruit-like aroma filled his nostrils.

CHAPTER TWENTY-EIGHT

CARA FOREST
THE KINGDOM OF VANDOLAY
1260 CE

Orlynd had grown increasingly uneasy about letting the king wander off alone. He convinced the king's guards to go back with him and find Déor.

"Yir Majesty!" Orlynd exclaimed. The warlock quickly jumped down from his horse and lowered his hood, revealing uneasy eyes.

"The king's been injured," stated Tierney, turning his attention to the blood seeping from Déor's tunic. "Your Majesty. Can you hear me?"

"Let's huv a look," Orlynd said.

Déor groaned.

Tierney watched as Déor took in a painful breath and slowly opened his eyes.

He said nervously, "Forgive me, Your Majesty. Your clothing must be unfastened in order to treat your wound. Will you permit us to assist you?"

"Granted," Déor whispered.

Tierney was gentle, but quick. He gasped when a deep gash was revealed. "In the name of the gods what could have caused this?"

"Look! In his hand, there's an arrow!" exclaimed Aindrias. "Someone's deliberately caused His Majesty harm."

Orlynd ripped off a piece of material from his robe's sleeve and handed it to Tierney. "Keep pressure oan it," Orlynd instructed. Orlynd then examined the arrow.

The blood is the colour of metal.

He ripped off another piece of material from his sleeve and wrapped it around the arrow. He lifted the arrow close to his nose.

Nae odour.

"Your Grace!" exclaimed Aindrias. "I beg of you. Tell us who did this. We will find the villain and see that he or she meets swift justice."

Déor blinked. He felt frightened, but he couldn't recall why or why they were there. Then the king recalled his grim circumstances.

Spirit…Eoghan…arrow…

Déor opened his mouth to speak, but his words were incomprehensible. He began to breathe rapidly in a panic.

Orlynd abruptly dropped the arrow. "Calm, Yir Majesty. Speak nae. Save yir strength."

"Or," Déor whispered.

"Ah'm here," Orlynd said, taking Déor's hand.

"Orlynd," Déor said, shivering violently.

"Hold oan, Yir Majesty!" Orlynd insisted. He placed a cool hand over Déor's brow and could feel the onset of fever. Whatever was ailing the king was quickly getting worse. With a voice of determination, Orlynd spoke, "If yis need tae tell me anything, look into ma eyes, n say it wi yir mind."

With the last of Déor's strength, he obeyed and fixed his gaze upon Orlynd for as long as he could.

THE PREVIOUS events from Cara Forest filled Orlynd's mind. He saw a man carrying bow and arrow, dressed in simple peasant's tunic with a rope around his waist. Orlynd watched as Eoghan lowered his bow and walked up directly to Déor and pushed the arrow further into his body.

"Long live the King!"

The scene went dark and transformed. Orlynd found himself in Coinneach Castle in King Francis's bedchamber. Before him was the king's massive ornately carved wooden bed, and on the floor on the foreside of the bed, lay the King Francis's body. A metallic liquid was still trickling out of the corners of his mouth.

The young prince knelt beside his father's body and wept, saying, "Father, wake up!"

"Ah'm sorry, Yir Grace," Orlynd said as he reached out to comfort the young prince.

However, Prince Déor aggressively pushed him away. "Don't touch me!" he said, turning around, tears falling down his face. There was a mix of pain and anger in his voice.

"It's all your fault! You should have known! You only had one responsibility, to protect my father, and be his soothsayer. But you couldn't do that, could you, because you are a liar and a fake!"

"Yir Grace, Ah tried."

"What use are you to me? Just looking at you disgusts me! Now, get out of my sight before I throw you out!"

ORLYND FOUND himself in the present. The king had lost consciousness. As he stared into Déor's face, he realised history was trying to repeat itself. "Ah failed yis last time, Yir Grace. Ah warned yir father, but he dinnae listen. Ah promise Ah won't fail yis this time."

"I found foot tracks going the opposite direction," Tierney interjected. "I'm sure I can catch whoever did this on horse."

"No!" shouted Orlynd, his gaze fixed back on the wound.

They both looked at Orlynd with confusion.

"Oor king has been poisoned," Orlynd announced. He turned to Aindrias and Tierney. "Tierney, yis shall git back tae the festivities n inform Her Majesty whit has happened here."

"Yes, Orlynd," Tierney answered. He watched Orlynd reach into his robe and bring out his wand.

"And what about you?" Tierney asked.

"Ah'm taking Déor tae Aracelly. There's only wahn person who can help him now," Orlynd replied, climbing onto his horse. He glanced down at Aindrias. "Help me git him oan tae ma horse."

"I shall accompany you. It is my duty to protect the king," Aindrias said.

"Nae," Orlynd protested, "We will be able tae travel much faster if it is jist oan horse."

Aindrias nodded, lifting Déor towards Orlynd, who wrapped his arms around Déor in order to keep him from falling. "Thair healer, Liliana de Caitie, can save his life. Thit Ah'm certain." Orlynd's expression showed determination. "The days ay the prophecy shall commence. It has been foretold."

CHAPTER TWENTY-NINE

COINNEACH CASTLE
THE KINGDOM OF VANDOLAY
1260 CE

Night had fallen, and the banquet hall of Coinneach Castle was filled with guests celebrating the day's festivities. Witches and warlocks from the Kingdom of Aracelly, and men from the Kingdom of Vandolay and Glendalow attended.

The queen's court enjoyed dancing to the fiddler's music while other guests enjoyed food and wine. All seemed to be genuinely pleased to be in attendance, except for the queen.

"His Majesty has still not returned from the royal hunt," chided Ciarán, sitting to the left of his daughter. "Certainly, he will be disappointed to be missing all these celebrations in his honour."

"Is that worry I hear in your tone?" mocked Anya. She sneered. "I am certain my husband will not be delayed much longer. Tell me, what news of Glendalow?"

"The plan has been a success. The potato crops are turning black and shrivelling up in Deermid's Fields. Even the ones that looked salvageable have gone bad. I sent word that the king was displeased with their inability to properly grow their crops and as a result has raised their taxes."

Anya, most pleased at the news, nodded her head slowly.

"However, the people have objected. There is talk if Déor doesn't change his mind, they will revolt."

"Then we shall teach these worthless peasants that when they disobey their king, there will be further consequences," Anya stated. She leaned back into her chair and grinned. "If they don't want to pay taxes, then their contribution to Déor's tribute will be increased by 10 percent."

"The crops are already failing; how will the people be able to give more?"

Before the steward could protest further, Anya raised her hand to silence him.

"They will simply have to work harder and plant more. And if they should choose to refuse again, the tribute will keep increasing until there is no food left and they have no choice but to sell their belongings, as well as their children off as slaves, in order to survive," she continued.

"Forgive me, Anya, but why?"

"You will never address me in such an informal way ever again. I am not just some commoner. I am your Queen!" She leaned in close to her father. She paused, laughed to herself and backed away so no one would notice the conflict. She calmed herself. "Perhaps, I had not made myself clear. You may be the steward, and my father, but that does not make you indispensable. Do not think I cannot strip you of your title and banish you from my court."

"You wouldn't dare," Ciarán objected. "You easily forget you wouldn't be the queen if I hadn't convinced Chancellor O'Brien you were a worthy suitor for His Majesty's son. King Francis would have looked elsewhere for a bride for his son."

"Well, now," she mocked. "King Francis is no longer the king, is he?" She smiled mischievously and then laughed.

Suddenly a loud commotion came from the entrance of the banquet hall.

"Your Majesty! Your Majesty!" exclaimed Tierney as he quickly made his way through the crowd towards the queen. The guests were shocked by this intrusion upon the celebration. Some protested loudly while others simply shook their heads.

"What is the meaning of this interruption?" Anya asked.

"Forgive me, Your Grace," said Tierney, lowering himself to the ground. "I come to you in haste with terrible news."

Anya looked at him with anticipation. Her heart began to race. Had her plan to kill the king been successful?

"What is it, Tierney? Speak."

Tierney took a deep breath and gazed up at Anya. "We were on the hunt in Cara Forrest. Déor became separated from us."

"What happened, Tierney? Stop biting your tongue. What are you not telling me?"

Tierney looked directly into Anya's eyes. "A man came out of the forest and shot the king with an arrow. Déor's been poisoned."

Anya stood abruptly. The crowd gasped. She stared forward, displaying no inkling that she already knew of the foul plot to kill the king. Anya swallowed, held her head high, and raised her hand to silence the crowd.

"Thank you, Tierney. We will find who is responsible for this crime and see that justice prevails." She slowly approached Tierney as the crowd bowed. "I seek an audience with you and the steward in my private apartment immediately," she stated. She then addressed her guests. "I bid the rest of you goodnight."

MCKINNON ESTATE
GLENDALOW
1260 CE

"IS THERE anything else I can get for you, Monsieur McKinnon?" Armand asked as he brushed a cool wet cloth against the old man's heavily wrinkled, feverish face.

"Yes," Mortain answered with a raspy voice. He reached forward with a shaky hand as he tried to sit up.

Seeing he was too weak to do it himself, Armand approached the bed and assisted the doctor.

"Please fetch Mierta," Mortain said between breaths. "Quickly! I...must...speak with him," he took a deep breath and coughed several times. "Need...to...tell him. Be quick," he uttered trying to calm his rapid breathing. "He is...in the cellar."

"Oui, Monsieur. I'll fetch him right away," Armand said, carefully helping the doctor reposition comfortably in his sickbed.

"My quill!" Mortain gasped. "No time. Need...my quill."

As soon as Armand had left the room, Mortain went into a coughing fit. He felt something warm and moist escape his lips and get caught in his beard. When he looked down towards his pillow, he also saw several drops of blood.

COINNEACH CASTLE
THE KINGDOM OF VANDOLAY
1260 CE

"TIERNEY, TELL me everything you know," commanded Anya.

"Of course, my queen," Tierney replied, then hesitated. He contemplated informing her about Déor's strange behaviour prior to the attack but decided not to.

"Well?" said Anya.

"Yes, so sorry, my queen," Tierney apologised. He cleared his throat. "The king stated there was a man dressed in a peasant's tunic with a rope tied around his waist."

The steward instantly recognised the man's description.

"Your Majesty," he began, "the man he speaks of is a resident of Glendalow. His name is Eoghan. He is a brigand. He is already wanted for looting. He has also been accused of being connected to an unsolved crime involving a witch who was murdered in a back-alley twenty-five years ago."

Anya turned to her father and raised an eyebrow. "Yes, I am familiar with him. He has already had previous trouble with the crown for poaching red deer in Cara Forest." She then turned back to Tierney. "Please, continue."

"Yes, Your Majesty." He cleared his throat again. "Eoghan flanked the king, using the fog to his advantage, and shot him."

Anya nodded with understanding. "And Eoghan? Was he captured?"

"No, my queen. He escaped through the forest."

"I see," Anya said as she walked towards the windows. "And where is the king now?"

"With the warlock Orlynd, my queen. They are going to Aracelly."

Anya turned suddenly. "To Poveglia, I assume?"

"Yes, my queen."

Anya clenched her fists but was careful not to display too much emotion. She relaxed her fists and smiled at Tierney. "I am pleased His Majesty is getting treatment. I am certain he will be cured. The Kingdom of Aracelly has the best healers. If anyone can save the king, it will be their healer, the witch, Liliana. I've been informed her skills are legendary." She then turned back to her father. "I require the assistance of your new potion maker."

"Your Majesty?" Ciarán questioned. "Forgive me. I do not have a potion maker."

"Oh, that's right, I hadn't informed you. That job has recently been filled. Mierta McKinnon will now be serving Glendalow and

Vandolay. As you may recall, his father has served as court physician for many years, and lucky for us, Mierta has inherited his father's talents. I could not envision anyone else being more capable."

"Your Majesty has chosen well," Ciarán replied.

"I'm glad you approve," Anya responded. "Tell him he is to construct a truth serum for me. The information Eoghan provides him would not normally be disclosed. However, I trust his skills will force Eoghan to admit his guilt, and we will be able to quickly proceed with his execution."

"As you wish. I will send a messenger to his residence as soon as I return to Tarloch Castle."

"Excellent," Anya answered. She waited until the steward had left the room. She then looked Tierney straight in the eyes.

"I have a request of you that I also hope you will accept."

"Anything, my queen."

"Round up some of our best soldiers and make way to Glendalow and arrest the brigand." Anya reached into a dresser drawer and pulled out a small pouch containing money. "For your trouble."

"You are very generous, Your Majesty," Tierney said.

Anya smiled again. "And don't forget that," she said, making a small twirl. "Thank you, Tierney. Now, please, leave me."

Once Tierney had left, Anya collapsed onto her couch. At that very moment she realised her plan had backfired. Instead of eliminating the king, she had only quickened the timing of the prophecy. Everyone knew of the prophecy: a person of royalty would fall in love with a resident of the Kingdom of Aracelly, resulting in not one, but two, identical heirs. This would bring forth the beginning of a dark period to all the kingdoms. And most importantly, her reign would be over.

"No," she sobbed.

Rage filled her heart. She would see that the prophecy would not come true. If she had to kill Déor and his future concubine, she would.

She picked up her hand mirror and smashed it across the table. Then she knocked the table and its contents onto the floor.

At the same time, several soldiers who stood guard in the hall outside the queen's private apartment tried their best to not show any reaction, completely oblivious of the real reason Anya was upset.

As each smash became louder, they couldn't help but cringe.

CHAPTER THIRTY

MCKINNON ESTATE
GLENDALOW
1260 CE

In the cellar Mierta quickly prepared a mixture in his flask, calculating the proper amount of ingredients. He had just finished pouring it accidentally into the wrong cauldron when he heard Lochlann's voice from the top of the stone stairs.

"Mierta? Are you down there?" Lochlann called.

Mierta turned just in time for the contents in the cauldron to erupt all over his freshly cleaned royal blue robe. He stared towards the direction of the staircase with a very irritated expression.

"Yes, I'm down here!" he shouted.

The noise from Lochlann's footsteps became louder as they echoed against the stone steps. Lochlann could hear Mierta swear between moments of self-inflicted pain while he worked unsuccessfully to remove remnants of the potion from his hair without burning himself.

He stopped on the bottom step, catching a glimpse of Mierta removing his soiled robe and tossing it into a corner. Lochlann raised an eyebrow and covered his mouth, trying not to chuckle at Mierta's predicament.

Mierta pretended to ignore Lochlann. He unfastened the belt around his long, cream coloured tunic, allowing it to fall against the floor. He lifted his tunic over his head. Patches of skin that had already changed over to an angry pink were revealed.

Lochlann cleared his throat. "We need to talk," he stammered.

Mierta grimaced in pain, walking over to the corner to deposit his tunic alongside his robe. He returned to one of his workbenches that had various ingredients perfectly organised in front of him. He started the potion again, this time working only in his breeches.

"Mierta are you listening to me?" Lochlann uttered with a tone of irritation. "For God's sake, do you not have a change of clothes around here?"

Mierta whirled toward him, his upper lip curving. The lighting hit Mierta's face just right to emphasise the few veins that could be seen on the left side of his face where scar tissue had formed. His eyes looked frightening, like they could pierce Lochlann's soul at that very moment. "I will find a change of clothes as soon as I have removed these burning chemicals from my skin, or have you failed once again to notice I've had a slight accident!"

"My apologies," Lochlann responded, intimidated. "I shall fetch you some clothes from upstairs."

Mierta continued to intently stare at his brother until he disappeared into the staircase.

Idiot.

He walked over to the cabinet and pulled out a small vessel of salve to help with the burns. He carefully applied the ointment between several intakes of sharp breath.

Shortly afterward, Lochlann returned, holding a long and fancy silk crimson tunic. Mierta reached out for it, taking it from Lochlann a bit aggressively. He did not thank him for the attire. Mierta rolled up the sleeves and walked back to the workbench to stir his potion.

"Now, you wanted to talk, yes? Well, I'm very busy. I need to calculate the correct ingredients."

"It's about the queen," Lochlann nervously confessed. "I did something I am not proud of and I am desperately in need of your guidance. I believe I—no, we—may be in danger."

This news caught Mierta's attention and he abruptly stopped preparing the potion. He adjusted his black breeches. "Danger? What kind of danger? What have you done?" He paused and tried to retain his focus. He picked up a small vial of clear liquid and poured it into a flask, causing chemicals to bubble and sizzle into the air.

Lochlann swallowed hard and then continued. "Anya persuaded me to deliver some type of poison to a brigand in Glendalow. I believe his name was Eoghan. Anya was attempting to create some kind of setup so Déor could be eliminated during the royal hunt. She implied you were the one who created the poison for her!"

"Poison?" he asked, already predicting what Lochlann's next question would be.

Worry filled Lochlann's voice. "Please, I beg of you, tell me it's not true."

Mierta thought for a moment, then answered slowly, as if hesitant. "Poison? Why, yes, I do recall making a poison for the queen."

"Mierta, I fear we will lose our heads. Everyone will know it was us!" Lochlann exclaimed.

Mierta laughed with amusement and turned around. "Oh, Lochlann. You, my brother, are a fool." He grinned and turned back to his potion. "What I meant to say is I did provide a poison for the queen, but it wasn't my concoction."

"Then why would she say you had?"

Mierta spoke towards the table with a bit of a snarky tone. "How else do you think the late king died?"

Lochlann's face turned pale. "I don't understand," he muttered.

Mierta spun around, approached Lochlann and wrapped an arm around him. "Why, of course you do. Quit your gawking and listen to me. Remember the stories growing up? Once upon a time, King Francis, one late, cold night went to his bedchamber not feeling well," he said, continuing the story while gesturing with his right hand. "He proceeded to undress when suddenly he saw something—a white form, or so he thought it was. It was actually a hallucination."

He paused, changing the inflection of his voice, and making it sound quieter. "The king glanced forward. He pointed towards the spirit. His pulse raced and his pupils dilated." Mierta raised his voice. "'Be gone, you despicable creature!'" He paused. "As soon as he uttered these last words, Francis gripped his chest, unable to catch his breath, and fell to the floor, dead." Mierta let go of Lochlann and immediately slapped his hands together. "His heart would beat no more, and yet there still was blood dripping out of his mouth. The end. Or was it? Ha!" Mierta turned back to his potions, an expression of achievement filled his face.

At that moment Lochlann had a realisation. "Rumours stated King Francis had died of fright, but what you are saying is that he was poisoned?!"

"Precisely," Mierta answered, his eyes beaming. "Anya wants Déor dead and will do whatever she needs to in order to see it come to be. All she requested of me was I give her poison in exchange for some new test subjects. Understand, this was the same poison that had previously been used in the castle, but what Anya didn't know was what I had given her wasn't fully effective."

Lochlann looked at Mierta disapprovingly.

Mierta's jaw opened and his face showed disgust. "Did you honestly think I was that stupid?" Mierta took a moment to compose himself before he started speaking again, this time with confidence. "Even if her plan should fail, and trust me, it will fail, as my elixir wasn't fully potent. But, it still will cause His Majesty to become very ill. There is a chance he could still die, and then there will be trouble.

Oh yes, there will be lots of trouble, but you, my brother, will come through for her in the very end. Why? Not because you are desperate for her love or affection," he teased, "but because you are destined for greatness."

Lochlann huffed. "Do not flatter me. I do not have the talent to create potions. I could be the advisor to the king and queen, but I am not a soothsayer. And I do not have the discipline to master the dark arts like you have. There's no way I can be intended for greatness when I do not even have power."

"Ah, power can be a tricky thing," Mierta answered, as he stirred his liquid. "Anya seeks it, desires it in fact, to conquer and rule the world." He then poured a small amount of potion into a small culture tube and drank some of it. He licked his lips. "Mmm, that is brilliant." He set down the culture tube, and then cleared his throat. "What Anya needs are subjects that will never betray her and do whatever she commands." He twiddled his fingers. "I reckon we can manoeuvre right into Anya's plan unsuspected," Mierta muttered to himself.

"Pardon?"

Mierta stopped. He began to laugh to himself. "Blimey! The solution couldn't be clearer!"

He turned to Lochlann and smirked. He wrapped his arm around Lochlann again and continued to speak, gesturing with his free hand.

"You will continue to aid Her Majesty, and I will continue to train you. But, in exchange for taking Déor's life, you will demand Anya makes you her new king."

"Me? King? But that's impossible! My blood is not of a royal. I can never be king," replied Lochlann.

Mierta covered Lochlann's mouth. "That's not the point. Laws can be rewritten," Mierta said. "Especially when it involves a Dark Lord." He winked, releasing Lochlann.

"I don't understand. Who's a Dark Lord?" questioned Lochlann.

Mierta became distracted by the sound of someone stumbling over a rat on the stairs.

"Never mind. Shh," he said, gesturing with his hand. "We are not alone." They heard the sound of a rat screeching at the indignity of its tail having been stepped on.

Mierta glimpsed back at Lochlann, nodded, and proceeded to point towards the entrance.

"Who's there?" Mierta called to the room. "Show yourself!"

Mierta and Lochlann stood and listened again.

Mierta tilted his head when he heard the sound of feet running back up the stairs. Someone had just overhead something they shouldn't, and Mierta was determined to stop the intruder. Lochlann turned to follow, but Mierta stopped him, raising a finger to his lips. He lowered his finger and raised his wand, positioning it at the ready, and chanted, *"Zapídra contrarium!"*

A yelp was heard followed by a loud thud as the intruder's legs became hard and immobile as stone.

CHAPTER THIRTY-ONE

MCKINNON ESTATE
GLENDALOW
1260 CE

Mierta slowly approached the intruder from behind. He reached down and flipped the man onto his back. He stared into the face belonging to his father's servant. "Ah. Armand. I suppose you overheard our entire conversation."

When Armand's eyes betrayed him, he opened his mouth to object, but Mierta replied, "No, don't say anything. That wasn't a question." He then pointed his wand towards Armand's chest.

Armand fearfully looked up at Mierta.

"You see, with just a slight wave of my wand I could stop your racing heart. Allow me to demonstrate." He gestured with his wand then focused on Armand's chest. *"Sin pectora."*

Armand grimaced as he felt his body grow heavy and pain filled the centre of his chest. He looked directly into Mierta's face as

Armand raised a hand towards his body. It felt like the inside of his body was being squeezed together.

"Yes, you are already experiencing what it feels like to have your life fade before your eyes. Your body becomes so overwhelmed that your heart literally stops while you still have perfect blood flow."

Armand opened his mouth, desperate to take in a deep breath, but he could not make his lungs obey him.

Mierta paused, almost enjoying the exhibition a little too much as he watched Armand struggle. He then thought better of it. "But I won't kill you. No. Not yet." He sighed and said, *"Pectora cepus,"* before lowering his wand.

Armand gasped again. He proceeded with a coughing fit, this time successfully forcing several breaths of air into his aching lungs until his heart returned to a normal beat.

"I reckon you will be more useful to me alive," Mierta said. He turned around and began to walk away as he placed his wand back in his breeches. Abruptly he twirled around. "I will tell you exactly how we are going to proceed, and I can promise you this: it is not going to end well for you." He looked away and frowned. "Which is quite the shame because I really liked you…until you decided to betray me. You have always been loyal and faithful to my family." He smiled. "But, you, I have a much better use for you. Yes!" He spun around. "You shall be my volunteer. I have to know if the spell actually works."

Lochlann looked confused. "But you just said he would be more useful alive?"

Mierta turned to the warlock. His face showed disappointment as he awkwardly gestured with his hands. "Who said I was going to kill him?" He lowered his hands and gave himself a moment to calm. "Trust me, Lochlann, Armand is not going to reveal it was my poison, which was given to you on orders of Her Majesty the queen," Mierta declared.

"Traitors! Your heads shall roll for your treachery," Armand cried out. "You will pay for plotting to kill the king!"

Mierta's jaw opened. He pointed a finger towards Armand. "That is a load of bollocks. Lochlann, my brother, did you just hear what he called us?"

"But, he's right. We are traitors, are we not? We're both going to lose our heads for this!" Lochlann cried.

"Relax, Lochlann." Mierta smirked. "Armand will not betray us, will you Armand?"

Armand looked dumbfounded at first, then shook his head rapidly, thinking it might be a good idea to play into their plan for the moment.

"Good. Now, prove to Lochlann I am correct and that you will still serve me by taking off your shirt."

"Pardon, good Monsieur?" questioned Armand.

"You heard me. Go on then. Do as I say, and take off your shirt, or I shall get very cross!" Mierta said, emphasising the last word. He frowned and continued, "I promise I will be done with you soon, and then you can be off doing whatever you were doing, like helping my father get to Poveglia."

Armand was stunned.

"You didn't think I already knew of father's plan, did you?"

"Hang on," Lochlann interrupted. "Father's ill? Since when?"

Mierta glanced over to Lochlann and gave him a look that had "you can't be serious" written all over it.

"He'll be all right, yes?" Lochlann questioned.

Mierta softened his face and stared at the ground. "Father is already too far gone." He looked up at Lochlann regretfully. "He is dying of Shreya. He'll never make it there. I'm sorry. He didn't want you to know."

"But, you can cure him, can't you?" He got up close enough to Mierta to appear threatening. "Can't you?!"

"No," Mierta answered. "I have been trying to create a cure, but I have been unsuccessful. The only thing that can possibly help him is performing a pneumothorax technique and putting his sick lungs to rest. However, the fact remains is that we've all been exposed. Even I have become infected."

Lochlann stood back and looked Mierta over. "That's impossible! You aren't showing any symptoms."

"It matters not. It's too late for me, but not for you. You both need to leave until the plague has passed. I shall write the queen, requesting she find a place at court for you lot." He paused, then abruptly tilted his head, brought it back and shook it, becoming irritated by Lochlann's ability to distract him. He turned to Armand. "Now, back to business. Take off your shirt or I'll be forced to hurt you."

Armand hesitated until Mierta had removed his wand from his breeches and had started to twirl it in his hand, waiting for Armand to obey him. Armand's fingers fumbled as he unbuttoned each of the buttons on his wool shirt and removed it, tossing it aside.

"Good. Now, lay back," Mierta commanded and positioned his wand in front of him.

Armand swallowed hard and then obeyed. He breathed in quickly. His racing heart could be seen each time his chest rose and fell.

Mierta smiled with satisfaction. "Ah. You see, Lochlann," he said as he strutted toward Armand. "You can't be a king without an army." He pointed his wand again towards Armand's heart.

Armand responded by clenching his fists tight and closing his eyes. He had no idea if what was to occur next would be painless, if Mierta would follow through and actually kill him this time, or if it would be something utterly excruciating.

"And you can't have an army without subjects that will obey your every word." Mierta looked up and stepped aside, presenting Armand with his wand. "Lochlann, I gift to you, your new second in command." He turned back to Armand, *"Curtreforéa draco machado!"*

Armand's eyes flew open and his back arched. He screamed at the top of his lungs. He was experiencing the most horrific burning sensation he had ever felt in his life.

Mierta beamed as he admired his own work while Lochlann stood next to him horrified.

"Mierta. Mierta, stop this madness!" Lochlann exclaimed. "You are not yourself!"

"I'm quite the opposite, Lochlann. You forget my wand's core contains a werewolf claw, which allows me to master transfiguration. Behold!"

Lochlann turned just in time to watch the appearance of a dark blue circular tattoo forming onto the surface of Armand's left shoulder. It continued to form until another image appeared, taking the shape of a magnificent red dragon engulfed by flames. The tattoo quickly came to life as the dragon's head tilted back and roared, matching Armand's cries.

CHAPTER THIRTY-TWO

MCKINNON ESTATE
GLENDALOW
1260 CE

W hat is that?" Lochlann nervously asked. He had seen Mierta experiment hundreds of times on innocent creatures, sometimes out of curiosity, most times to see how much they could tolerate various spells of torture, but he never had he seen him perform on a live human being. He was beginning to believe that his brother was slowly descending into madness.

"*That*, my brother, is a brand," Mierta stated between smiles, placing his wand back into a pocket of his breeches. He watched Armand arch his back, screaming and squirming like a bug trying to get away after being caught up in a spider's web.

Lochlann nodded, though not completely convinced. "What does it do, then?"

"Ah. It's really an easy spell, actually. It's a mind-binding spell. It makes its bearer lose all of his or her free will," Mierta explained.

"How does it work?" Lochlann asked.

"It activates when the brain receives a sudden burst of...Oi!" He frowned, marching up to Armand. He observed Armand's entire body twitch. Mierta decided to speak down to him. "Now, I really enjoy a good sound of screaming, but could you stop it now? It really is quite distracting!"

When Armand didn't obey, Mierta gestured with his arms and hands. "Oh, come on, it doesn't hurt *that* much. Quit the dramatics and be quiet!"

Almost instantly, Armand recovered from the shock to his system.

Pleased, Mierta said, "There, that's better. Breathe normally. You are all right now. Go on, then. Put your shirt back on. But, first," he once again revealed his wand and pointed it towards Armand's legs, "*Zapídra contrarium!*"

Armand regained the ability to move his legs.

"You can stand up now," Mierta said, putting his wand away.

Armand stood as commanded; his movements were slow and stiff, and his eyes looked like he was in some kind of trance-like state.

Mierta grinned, then twirled around and turned his attention back to Lochlann. "Now, as I was saying," he walked back towards Lochlann and put his arm around him. "Mind-bending spell: it activates when the brain receives a sudden burst of psychic transmissions. Those who are branded have absolutely no control of their actions. Here," Mierta pulled Lochlann over to Armand, eager to show him the signs of his success. "Look at his eyes."

Armand winced when he began to button his shirt.

"Ah. Yes. Sorry. I forgot to mention to be careful when you button up. The brand will sting." He laughed in amusement, then turned Armand around and forced him to look at them. Mierta pointed. "Now, Lochlann, notice how the eyes have gone dull. Blimey, it's an amazing process. His brain is, at this very moment, desperately trying to fight against its new controller, only it can't. He can't resist you."

"What do you mean?"

"What I mean to say is *you* control the brand. You could order him to do anything, anything at all, and no matter how he truly feels about the situation, he will do whatever you desire. For example," Mierta turned and frolicked back to the wooden bench. He grabbed some new ingredients, started up a new cauldron, brought it to a boil and then grabbed a new small culture tube and poured some of the solution into it while Lochlann watched in amazement. He was eager to prove to Lochlann just how powerful this spell really was. He returned to Lochlann and Armand. He held the small culture tube in front of Lochlann. "Here. Tell him to drink this. He has absolutely no idea what is in my concoction, but I can assure you he will drink it."

Lochlann swallowed hard. He was growing more uncomfortable the longer he stayed. "But what if I don't want him to do it?"

"Do you not trust me?" Mierta frowned. "If you truly believe you are my apprentice and I am your master, then you must continue to listen to me and do as you're told. Go on now, tell Armand to drink that."

Lochlann cleared his throat and nodded his head. "All right then. Show me that what Mierta says is true," he took the small culture tube from Mierta's hand and held it in front of Armand. "Will you drink this if I tell you to?"

At that very moment, Mierta locked eyes with Armand's, his glance piercing Armand's soul. Lochlann had no idea the true command was coming directly from Mierta to Armand using only his mind.

"Oui, good Monsieur, I must. It is your will," Armand responded obediently.

He reached for the small culture tube and took it from Lochlann's hand.

"No, wait!" Lochlann said. "It isn't my will."

Before Lochlann could finish his sentence, Armand bent his head back and drank the solution.

Lochlann's face turned to horror. He realised in his heart at that very moment, he had actually wanted Armand to drink the potion. Was he becoming evil? He had no idea what was in the solution. For all he knew, Mierta had only been using Armand as a way to eliminate him from revealing any of the information he may have overheard, and he, Lochlann, had just fallen into the trap.

"Ha!" Mierta clapped, bringing Lochlann back from his thoughts. He strutted over to Lochlann. "Brilliant, what a very clever way to make an order. You wanted to see what would happen and you got your wish. Now, what will be the result, hmmm? Will he die? Will he turn into some fascinating creature?"

Lochlann could only stare at Armand, afraid and curious at the same time.

However, before he could answer, Mierta took over the conversation. "Relax. All he drank was some truth serum. I decided I better start working on one for Anya when she sends for my presence, and believe me, if what you told me was the truth, she will, once this brigand, Eoghan, is caught." He spun around. "Now, there is one other thing you must understand, and understand it well. Armand will be forever loyal to you. He will never betray you, and he will always do what you ask." He turned back to Armand, who no longer looked to be caught in any kind of spell. "For example: tell me, Armand, who do you serve?" Again, he made persuasive eye contact.

"The warlock, Lochlann, good Monsieur," Armand answered.

No. This cannot be, Lochlann thought.

Mierta smiled, further pleased at himself.

"But, what if I don't want him to serve me? I can't force him, that's not me. I beg of you Mierta, how do I break the brand?"

Mierta laughed. He began to strut away, his laughter becoming even more apparent. Then he became serious and turned back to Lochlann. "There is only one way to break the spell."

"And that is?" Lochlann asked desperately.

Mierta smirked then spoke matter-of-factly. "Your death."

Unbeknownst to them, at that exact moment, their father had gotten out of bed, desperate to find Mierta. Then a severe coughing attack racked his body, causing him to vomit a large amount of blood. He collapsed onto the floor. Dead. In his clenched hand was a letter revealing a disturbing secret he had been keeping most of his life.

CHAPTER THIRTY-THREE

CARA FOREST
THE KINGDOM OF VANDOLAY
1260 CE

Froebel! Ah goat tae help him," Orlynd mumbled, jolting awake and quickly sitting up. He took several quick breaths and attempted to calm his racing heart. He gazed around him with confusion.

He was still in the Cara Forest near the end of a red clay road he had been following by horse for several days.

It was now daylight, but he vaguely remembered setting camp the previous evening when fatigue overcame him, prohibiting him from being able to travel any further. He had made a small fire and had carefully positioned Déor against one of the trees in order to prevent him from injuring himself further.

The only sounds were of birds chirping, mosquitoes buzzing, and small animals scurrying through the underbrush.

Orlynd breathed a sigh of relief. He carefully reached up and touched his brow, noticing he was covered in a cold, damp sweat. He had had the dream again, only this time it hadn't felt like a dream. This time it had felt real.

Orlynd's mind flashed to Froebel as he lay dying in his twin brother's arms. He recalled his appearance. He had the same colour hair as Déor, and his twin, Friedrich, was dressed in the kingdom's royal attire and had Déor's eyes.

However, there was also a distinct difference. Never in the king's lineage had there been a warlock, and yet, in Friedrich's hand, had been a wand.

There was no doubt in his mind, the lad was a warlock and possessed the wand that belonged to Lady Liliana, the healer witch from Poveglia. Yet it was impractical. Based on the rules of the Rite of Wands, a wand could only serve one witch or warlock. It could never serve another. Which meant, yes, he was certain—Friedrich and Froebel, born of witch and man, had to be the king's heirs. But that didn't explain why they had been able to possess her wand. They were the mirror twins the prophecy spoke of. The prophecy had come true. And if this had been a true omen, their future was in peril. There was still a chance this future would not happen. Fate could be changed. This vision could never happen. This vision would not happen.

Determination filled Orlynd's heart. He would see to it that the royal line of Vandolay would remain safe, and he would start doing that by finishing the task before him—getting the king to Poveglia.

He stood up and began to walk towards Déor, slumped up against a tree. "Yir Majesty," whispered Orlynd. "Forgive me. Yis cannae continue tae sleep. We must be hasty n git yis tae Poveglia."

He gasped.

Déor's face was deathly pale and there was a blue tint around the corners of Déor's lips.

"Yir Majesty!" Orlynd exclaimed, quickly approaching him. He knelt down beside Déor and placed a cool hand against his brow.

The fever's getting worse.

"Forgive me, Yir Majesty. Ah hudnae even goat a deck at yir wound."

Carefully, Orlynd repositioned Déor onto his back. He unfastened Déor's tunic, unbuttoned his wool shirt, and opened it, so he could check the wound.

Orlynd's face turned grim. Déor's breathing had become shallow overnight, and the wound looked more metallic than ever. It also did not appear to be healing at all.

Orlynd placed a finger on Déor's neck and checked for a pulse. He sighed with relief to find a quick, though strong, heartbeat. Hope was not all lost. There was still time to get the king to Poveglia.

"No," whined Déor.

"Yir Majesty?" questioned Orlynd. "Can yis hear me?"

Déor let out a high-pitched squeal, which sounded like an old kettle about to boil and let off steam.

Before Orlynd's brain could register what was about to occur, Déor's body stiffened and began to convulse.

"Hang oan, Yir Majesty! Stay wi me!" shouted Orlynd. He quickly repositioned Déor onto his side. Tears fell down the warlock's cheeks.

It's ma fault. Ah've waited tae long. This fit may take him and thir is naught more Ah can dae tae help him.

Orlynd closed his eyes and prayed Déor would survive.

Shortly, the fit stopped and Déor's body relaxed. Orlynd opened his eyes and gently lifted his hands off the king. Anxiously, he reached up and checked for a pulse. Déor was still alive, though his pulse had gotten significantly weaker.

Orlynd stood up and readied his horse.

"Hang oan, Yir Majesty," Orlynd said, stomping out the fire. He turned and attempted to lift the king.

Blimey! He is heavier than Ah realised, Orlynd thought to himself.

He reached into his robe for his wand and pointed it at himself. *"Esallertis!"*

Feeling additional strength in his arms, he turned and easily lifted the king and positioned him back onto the horse.

"Thit's better," Orlynd said. He climbed onto the horse, placed his arms securely around Déor and grabbed the reins. "Stay wi me a little bit longer! Ah will git yis tae Poveglia!"

He then gently tapped his heel underneath the horse's stomach, commanding him to move.

As they approached the end of the forest, increasing patches of sunlight could be seen glimmering between the trees. Soon they were in the warm sun and on their way to the large wooden gate, which led into the eastern portion of the Kingdom of Aracelly.

The Kingdom of Aracelly was an enchanted kingdom, surrounded by a large river in the shape of an oval, believed by many to be the gateway to the heavens.

The eastern portion of the kingdom containing cobblestone streets and numerous stone buildings of the same height was where most business and entertainment took place.

The centre of the kingdom contained four main crossing points, each leading to a variety of other businesses including the sanatorium, Poveglia, which was home to its best healers, and the Draconiera Mountain, located on Draconiera Island in the middle of the harbour. Located directly south was a vast area of flatland, which served as home to many of its residents as well as a resource to grow food and raise animals. Directly to the east were miles and miles of farmland and different coloured cottages.

The gate hadn't always been there. Travellers used to be able to come and go through the kingdom as they pleased, but that was before the great purge.

The gate itself was very large and made of wood that was worn from years of exposure to the elements. At first sight it appeared to be solid, but on further inspection a small doorway could be seen in one corner.

As Orlynd reigned his horse to a stop he studied this small door and shouted, "Oan the orders ay His Majesty, the King ay Vandolay, Ah command yis tae open the gate!"

A short warlock with a bent back opened the door slightly, took a good look at Orlynd and then proceeded to close the door, only keeping it slightly ajar. He questioned. "And why would the King of Vandolay request entry into Aracelly, the kingdom of the warlocks?"

Orlynd took a deep breath and spoke a bit sternly. "Ah've come seeking aid fir the king. He has been poisoned n will die without help fi the healers ay Poveglia."

"I see. In bad shape, is he?" asked the gatekeeper.

Orlynd was quickly growing irritated by the delay. "Ah'm Orlynd fi Aracelly n Ah'm his advisor n soothsayer. It is ma sworn duty tae serve His Majesty. Now, delay me nae further n let me pass!"

The gatekeeper hesitated before replying, "Orlynd the soothsayer, we want no trouble here. How do I know that is the real King of Vandolay and not some imposter? You are not carrying the flag of the kingdom."

"Ah sent the king's guard carrying the flag back tae Coinneach Castle tae alert Her Majesty," Orlynd answered. He waited for the warlock to open the gate, but again, he did not. Orlynd had had just about enough. "If yis dinnae open the gate, Ah will smash it apart wi ma wand!" Orlynd asserted. "Ah'm Orlynd O'Brien, son ay..."

"O'Brien? Yes, I know who you are. Everyone here knows who *you* are. And it is my job to keep people like you on the outside," the gatekeeper answered.

Orlynd's eyes were full of fury. He didn't have time to argue. Déor needed help now! He held out his wand in the direction of the wooden gate and shouted, *"Obrate resillas!"*

The gatekeeper glanced towards the gate. Creaking wood and stressing hinges met his ears. He jumped out of the way before the gate was smashed to pieces.

Orlynd placed his wand back into his robe. "Ah says nae mair."

He held his eyes forward, taking a hold of the reins. He squeezed his thighs and gently kicked his horse, who protested with a neigh. They quickly proceeded through what remained of the gate and onwards towards the heart of the kingdom.

CHAPTER THIRTY-FOUR

POVEGLIA
THE KINGDOM OF ARACELLY
1260 CE

Y ou will be feeling much better now," Liliana stated to the young four-year-old warlock as the white light faded around his wrist.

"Thank you, Ms. Liliana," the warlock said, as he wiggled his newly healed wrist around and laughed with delight.

"You're welcome," Liliana smiled between laughs. She lowered her black wooden wand with a dark blue obsidian crystal connected to the shaft and proceeded to put it back into the small right front opening of her purple dress.

She moved strands of stray hair behind her ears. "Remember to be more careful when you play outside. Listen to your mother and keep yourself out of trouble."

The young warlock grinned and practically jumped down from his examination table. "I will, Ms. Liliana!"

Liliana nodded. "All right then. Off you go."

"Bye, Ms. Liliana and Ms. Elyse!" He waved at the young witch who had been helping the healer.

She watched as the young warlock left the room. She proceeded to sweep back her long, dark, wavy brown hair.

A few minutes later, she stopped and abruptly turned her head to the commotion coming from outside the building of Poveglia. Her blue-green eyes widened and her lips slightly parted as she listened to the noise outside growing more intense. She rushed to the window and glanced out to see a large crowd of witches and warlocks that had gathered. She looked a bit closer, her eyes growing wide, recognising the King of Vandolay slumped forward on his horse.

"Liliana, what is going on outside?" asked Elyse with a voice of worry.

Liliana turned. She took a deep breath to keep her composure. She then smiled gently and squatted to meet eye level with the young two-year-old witch.

"Lady Elyse," Liliana said, looking into the child's grey-blue eyes as she laid her hands on the young witch's shoulders. "Please go and find your grandmother. I must go address the crowd. Later, you can help me change a bandage, okay?" Liliana smiled.

The young witch smiled and nodded. She turned and ran off in search of her grandmother. Elyse's shoulder-length blonde hair shined against the lighting of Poveglia as she ran down the white marble hallway.

Liliana turned the opposite direction and slowly started to walk down the hall, her face growing more worried. She reached into her dress for her wand and raced towards the entrance of Poveglia.

× ✕ ×

WHEN LILIANA opened the door, she saw Orlynd had climbed down from his horse and was cradling Déor in his arms. Behind them a large crowd of witches and warlocks had gathered, some curious to see what was going on, while others seemed just as anxious as Orlynd. As Liliana made her way down a large flight of white marble stairs, her hair shimmered so intensely in the sunlight she could have been mistaken for an angel.

"What is the meaning of this? What has happened?" Liliana asked with an authoritative voice, lowering herself to the ground so she could examine the king.

"His Majesty was shot with an arrow in Cara Forest. It was poisonous," Orlynd explained with anxiety in his voice as Liliana loosened the king's tunic and wool shirt. He watched as Liliana pulled the piece of cloth used for bandages from Déor's chest and took an intense look at the wound near his breast.

"*Strychnos toxifera*," Liliana uttered. "It is a plant often used to create poisonous darts and arrows. But how can this be? He should be dead already." She placed a finger over Déor's neck and felt a pulse that was quickly becoming weaker. "He is fading. The poison has already spread through his vital organs. Soon his lungs will be put to rest. He doesn't have much time left," she said, raising her wand and positioning it over the centre of his chest. She placed her other hand over Déor's forehead as she uttered, "*Emaculavi el curpas y mehartis!*"

Orlynd watched as a white healing light slowly absorbed into Déor's body, and Déor's breathing became stronger.

Amazed, Orlynd looked up at Liliana. He had heard many stories of her healing abilities, but he had never seen her up close before. He took a minute to study her features.

Liliana was an extremely beautiful young woman. She had a heart-shaped face and a mole located slightly to the right of her upper lip.

"Ah beg ay yis," Orlynd said unexpectedly, tears falling down his face as he looked up into Liliana's face. "Yis must save him. The future ay oor kingdoms depend oan it."

Liliana looked straight into Orlynd's eyes and spoke with a sassy voice. "Do not doubt my gift. I will save him!"

"Is everything all right, madam?" a warlock who had come down the stairs asked.

"Yes, Leon," answered Liliana still gazing at Orlynd. "Help me get the King of Vandolay into one of the sick rooms. Gather all of our advanced healers and instruct them to meet me there."

"Yes, Ms. Liliana," Leon replied. He moved towards Orlynd and carefully lifted the king into his arms.

Liliana waited till Leon had passed her by before turning around to proceed back up the stairs. Abruptly she stopped and looked back at Orlynd intently.

"Do not fear," Liliana said. "We will see to it your king's life is spared."

CHAPTER THIRTY-FIVE

MCKINNON ESTATE
GLENDALOW
1260 CE

Father? Armand informed me you wished to see me?" Mierta
said, taking a few steps into the room.

He glanced around and observed his father was no longer in
his sickbed. Fear filled his heart.

He turned back to Lochlann who had followed him up the stairs.
"No one is to enter this room but me," Mierta cautioned.

He could feel his pulse in his temples and sweat droplets starting to drip from under the pits of his arms. He crept over to the right
side of the bed and stopped. There was blood, lots of blood, and his
father's body lay on the ground.

"Mierta?" questioned Lochlann, entering the room. "What's
wrong?"

Hearing footsteps behind him, Mierta turned around, forcing Lochlann to stop. "Don't come any closer! Get out of here! Get out of here, now!" he exclaimed.

"Where's Father?" Lochlann asked, returning to the hallway. His body began to tremble. Something was wrong. "Mierta? Talk to me!"

"Shut up, and do not come any closer." Mierta turned around. He stood still staring down at his father's body. There was blood, far too much blood. There wasn't a doubt in Mierta's mind his father was dead. "He's over here," Mierta responded, fighting tears from forming.

"What? You mean, unconscious? Is he all right?"

Mierta took in a deep breath. He attempted to calm himself only it was useless.

"I do not know," Mierta answered, his voice breaking. "I'm going to have a look."

With dread, he slowly approached his father. Attentive of the blood, Mierta lowered to his knees. As he moved closer, he observed his father was still, positioned on his side. His eyes were open, but no movement could be seen. Mierta moved a hand to his mouth, arranging it into a fist, preparing himself for the worst. He placed a finger over his father's neck. The body was still warm, but there was no pulse.

No, Mierta thought.

He bowed his head while laying a hand over his father's shoulder. His father had gone to be reunited with his mother and the man his father considered to be his best friend.

"I'm sorry," Mierta whispered, tears rolling down his cheeks. "I'm sorry I failed you."

He had been so close to discovering a cure, but it hadn't been enough. Mortain had been too ill. Even so, he had failed. The future he had seen in his Rite of Wands was coming to pass. The last thing he had expected was that it would begin through his own family.

As he wept, he continued to look over his father's body. The front of his long white nightshirt was covered in blood. It looked as if his father had vomited and then died shortly afterward. The metallic cloying smell was filling the air. It reminded him of the time he had sliced open a piglet from the chest down in order to understand pain tolerance as it squealed in agony. He recalled wondering whether his had mother felt the same pain while she was being murdered.

Rage towards himself filled Mierta's mind. He had failed not only to save his mother, but now also his father.

Then, he noticed what looked like a crumbled piece of parchment sticking out of his father's hand.

Crinkling his brow, he carefully reached for the parchment, and smoothed it out in his hand. It had not been written too long ago for the ink had partially smeared; however, the writing was still legible.

It read: "His real name is Verlyn."

What? What kind of bollocks is this? Who is Verlyn? What were you going on about, Father? Mierta wondered.

"Father!" cried Lochlann, breaking Mierta's thoughts.

Hearing the sound of footsteps behind him, Mierta quickly reached into his pocket, turned around, flicked his wand and shouted, *"Vorbíllion!"*

Lochlann was lifted into the air and thrown rapidly backward against the wall. An audible, *"Oooof!"* escaped from Lochlann's lips as he fell to the floor like a statue being pulled down from its pedestal.

Not caring whether he had injured Lochlann, Mierta talked down to him. "I warned you...not to come in here. I do not understand why you refuse to listen! Do you not comprehend the words coming out of my mouth are important?!" There was an edge of pain in his voice. He paused, noticing Lochlann was not moving.

"Lochlann?"

Worry filled his face. His pulse was now throbbing in his ears. He quickly inhaled and exhaled a few times.

"Lochlann," he stammered, wiping tears from his face.

What have I done? I only meant to get him out of the room!

He rushed over to his brother. Keeping his grasp around his wand, he gently turned Lochlann onto his back. He looked down into Lochlann's pain-filled face, watching him desperately try to inflate his lungs.

"Lochlann, listen to me," Mierta began, regaining control. "Your diaphragm is paralysed. You cannot breathe, but it is only temporary. I will get you relief." He drew Lochlann's knees up to his abdomen. "Now, I need you slowly inhale through your nose, and exhale through your mouth. Go on then and do as I say."

Lochlann obeyed.

A few minutes later, his breathing steadied. Mierta checked his pulse, feeling it stabilise.

"There. That better?" He smiled.

He began to stand when Lochlann revealed his wand from underneath his robe.

"*Palavaríso!*" shouted Lochlann, causing Mierta's wand to fly out of his hand and land directly behind him.

Mierta briefly stared at his empty hand before looking behind him, noting the location of his wand on the floor. He turned and looked back at Lochlann with bewilderment.

Lochlann has never been courageous enough to challenge me. Perhaps I misjudged him, and he isn't as incompetent as I had initially thought, Mierta concluded.

"What is your problem?" shouted Lochlann, holding his wand out towards Mierta. "You could have killed me!"

"I'm sorry. I lost control of my emotions," Mierta said, holding up both of his hands. "Please. Put your wand away!" Mierta watched Lochlann lower his wand and place it in a pocket of his breeches before he lowered his own hands. He looked Lochlann in the eye. His voice sounded hopeless. "He's dead, Lochlann. Father succumbed to the Shreya." His emotions were beginning to control him. "You must believe me. The longer you remain in his house the greater chance you will succumb to the same disease."

"I won't just leave you and Father behind," protested Lochlann.

"You have no choice!" shouted Mierta. "I will accept the task of burying his body."

"Mierta, you don't have to do this."

"Yes, I do. I told you before. I'm infected. Believe me, if anyone should make contact with the blood or merely inhale the particles from this room, they shall become infected, too!" Mierta answered, turning away. How long would it be before he started showing symptoms? A few days? A week?

"Mierta?" questioned Lochlann.

Mierta looked back at Lochlann. There was a look of fear in his eyes. "You must return to Coinneach Castle and warn the queen."

"Warn her of what?"

"Lochlann, I know you do not understand, but please try to follow, this is very important," Mierta replied. "Father told me he didn't just go to Edesia to visit his best mate. The disease was already there. Tiberius wrote him a letter, requesting he come to Norhamptone. He thought Father could help. By the time Father arrived, hundreds of people were infected. Tiberius was one of the first to succumb. That's how Father became infected." He paused. "Lochlann, the Shreya has come to Iverna. Please, I beg of you, take Armand and return to the Kingdom of Vandolay. Remember to stay in Anya's good graces and do whatever she asks. If we should survive, she may reward you with a title. Then our plan can proceed, and you will be closer to becoming king."

"But, what about you?" Lochlann asked.

"I must focus solely on my work. If I isolate myself, I may be able to conjure up a cure before..." He stopped. He half-smiled at Lochlann. "If anything you must understand, it is this. If I do not find a cure, my life is forfeit."

Lochlann approached Mierta and hugged him. "Now, you listen to me. You are the most talented warlock in all of Iverna. Father said you were a genius. I'm confident if anyone can conjure a cure, it will be you." He broke the hug and glanced at Mierta. "You aren't going to die."

Mierta nodded, though unconvinced.

"I will go to the Kingdom of Vandolay as you suggest. I shall go gather some things. Be well, my brother."

Mierta nodded again.

"Lochlann?" he said, looking away. "Please, apologise to the queen. Tell her I send my love and ask her for her forgiveness. I will be unable to perform my duty as her potion maker. Tell her I request she find a place for you and Armand in court."

"Of course."

He watched Lochlann leave the room.

A few minutes later, Mierta walked up to where his wand lay on the ground and picked it up. He studied it, confirming it had not taken any damage. He shrugged, placing it back into the pocket of his breeches. Defeated, he approached his father's bed and sat down on the edge. He pulled his hands up to his mouth and wept.

TO BE CONTINUED...

Author's Note

Thank you for spending your time reading the first book in The Rite of Wands series. If you enjoyed what you read, would you please leave a short review on your favourite online retail site?

The greatest compliment you can show an author is by leaving a review. It not only lets them know how much you appreciate their work, it also opens the opportunity for other readers to find and discover their next favourite book or series.

Thank you!

If you would like to join my mailing list to be notified of upcoming books and news, please visit my website at:

www.mackenzieflohr.com

Mackenzie

Acknowledgments

To the After Hours Writing Group, composed of Erin Eveland, R.A. Andrade, Shelly Towne, Lynn Parsons, Ted, and Matt Calabrese—for your insightful feedback and encouragement to keep writing, and to never give up!

To Max, for giving me the best writing advice anyone could have given—keep going back in the past.

To Aunt Carol, for the sleepless nights you spent critiquing my story like it was an Honour's English assignment, and for being honest when my writing needed improvement.

To Ivette Perez—for assisting me with the phonetics of my spells.

To Donna Lutkus-Phillips, for your assistance and endless patience of being my sounding board, and putting up with me when I would do nothing but obsessively ramble.

To my amazing editors, Lisa McNeilley and Morgan Smith, for your insightful knowledge, feedback, and leadership to help bring my vision to life.

To Jacquie New, my multi-talented proofreader. Thank you for being the perfectionist you are!

To my publisher BHC Press, you are the absolute best!

To the very talented Magical Alley for helping forge and bring to life Mierta's wand, and creating the coolest wand stand to coordinate.

To British actor, Matt Smith, for inspiring the creation of Mierta McKinnon. Without him, this series would have never existed. Swoosh!

About the Author

Mackenzie Flohr grew up in the heartland of America, chasing leprechauns and rainbows and dreaming of angels. Her parents nurtured a love of fantasy and make-believe by introducing her at a very young age to the artistic and cultural opportunities that the state of Ohio had to offer.

From the time she could hold a pencil, Mackenzie was already creating pictorial interpretations of classic stories, and by the age of nine, she and a childhood friend were authors and reviewers of their own picture books.

While following her love of adventure, Mackenzie found a second home, the Beck Center for the Arts Children's and Teen Theater School. It was there that a world of wonder was only a script and a performance away.

Yet it wasn't until she was on a trip to Indiana, viewing a Lord of the Rings exhibit, that the innermost desire of her heart became clear to her. She wanted to write a fantasy of her own, one that could inspire imagination in others and lead them into a magical world of their own making. She hopes The Rite of Wands will do just that.

Wherever we live and wherever we come from is our individual heartland. Anything is possible and everything can happen. Pure imagination is in all of us—we only need to discover it, and sometimes story telling helps.

Visit Mackenzie's website at
www.mackenzieflohr.com

CPSIA information can be obtained
at www.ICGtesting.com
Printed in the USA
LVHW040749100619
620693LV00001B/34